THE T.....
JENNY CRUMB

Martina Dalton

WRITE AS RAIN BOOKS

Martina Dalton

The Third Eye of Jenny Crumb

Cover Design by Martina Dalton
Cover Model, Madeline Dalton
Photo by Tammy Davison

First Edition, 2013
ISBN 978-0-9897221-1-7

Dedication

This book is dedicated to my family, who continued to encourage and believe in me even when I didn't believe in myself. They are the best.

Acknowledgements

My first novel, *The Third Eye of Jenny Crumb*, was a huge undertaking. I could not have written it without the help of so many amazing people. First and foremost, I'd like to thank my family, Matt, Madeline, and Kai, who put up with so much. They really went the extra mile for me.

My heartfelt thanks goes to my wonderful writing critique group, *Writers in the Rain*. They are not only the best critique partners a writer could have, but they are also dear friends. I love them all! Thank you, Angela Orlowski-Peart, Fabio Bueno, Eileen Riccio, Brenda Beem, and Suma Subramaniam from the bottom of my heart. I also wanted to extend a thank you to my lovely and talented editor, Alyssa Palmer. Thanks to my friend, Tammy Davison of Bella Photography, who took the beautiful photo for the cover. A warm thank you goes to my Girl Scouts, who lent me their names. Thanks also to the wonderful and gifted people who helped me learn about what true psychics go through every day. Char Sundust, Pamela Jensen, Roshi Paquin, and the late Dariusz Rawa. These beautiful people are the real deal and were so generous with their time.

And last, but not least, thanks to the really great people who read the novel during its first few drafts: my mom, Lindy Sutter, my sister, Marion Graves, and my friends, Lynn Muranaka, Deb Casper, Lisa Davenport, Aya Shimizu, Mallika Wagle, and Renee Gibbs. I'm sure I will call on them all to read my second novel, *The Sixth Sense of Jenny Crumb*. Get ready, guys!

Chapter 1

"Watch where you're going," a big guy wearing an oversized hoodie slurred as he bumped into me. The smell of alcohol wafted off of him. Wow, really? Drunk already? It wasn't even 7:30 in the morning yet. I moved away from the guy, eager to avoid him and his drunken haze.

A light drizzle fell from the Pacific Northwest sky. The sound of tires screeching and doors slamming echoed through the school parking lot. I shivered as I hurried through the throng of students, all headed for the big doors to Newport High School. I made it to the entrance and squeezed through into the commons with all the other students.

"I said, watch it!" Drunk guy once again bumped into me.

Flash.

His mom, on the couch, her arm hanging over the edge in slumber.

An empty bottle of Jim Beam was lying on the carpet beneath her outstretched hand.

"Sorry." I pushed the image out of my mind, and carefully avoided getting too close to him. He staggered away from me and bumped into someone else. I shook my head.

Going with the flow, I made it to my locker.

"Hi, Jenny." A girl appeared at my side. Her sparkly eye shadow reached up to the arcs of her eyebrows, and

1

overly bright highlights streaked her dark hair. A fake grin was plastered on her face.

"Uh, hi. It's Marcella, right?" I pulled a couple of books out of my bag and stashed them in my locker, then glanced at her.

"Yeah!" she said a little too brightly. "You remembered."

Flash.

I hate her. She has everything—just like all the other bitches on the team. But I need her to like me if I'm going to get on the squad.

I sighed, pushing her thoughts out of my head. My mind was cluttered with everyone else's feelings—it was hard enough to just have my own.

"What's up?" I tried to sound as polite as possible.

She flung her hair off her shoulder, and gave me a Crest 3D White Strip smile. "Hey, I'm having a party at my house this weekend. You're invited, of course. Do you think you could invite the other cheerleaders? Pretty much anybody who is anybody is going."

"Oh, okay. Sure, I'll invite them." Like hell I would.

"Thanks!" She turned on her heel and bounced off down the hall.

"What was that all about?" Julia's voice came from behind me.

I closed my locker. "That girl, Marcella, invited me... invited *us* to her party this weekend. I don't know why, though. I think she hates me."

"What gives you that idea?" Julia nudged me forward, and we made our way to our first period class.

"I don't know," I lied.

"Eh, she's just jealous of you. I wouldn't worry about it."

Just before we reached our classroom, a tall guy turned the corner ahead of us. He glanced down at the piece of paper he was holding.

"Hey, do you know where Room 106 is?" he asked.

Julia turned and pointed to the left. "Yeah, turn this way. It should be about two doors down."

"Thanks." He shifted his backpack strap on his shoulder and hurried down the hall.

"Who was that?" I asked.

"I don't know." Julia shrugged. "Some new guy."

"He's hot."

I watched him disappear into the classroom. Julia tugged on my arm. "Hurry up! We're going to be late."

***

Boom, boom, boom. I resisted the urge to cover my ears. "The bass is a little loud."

"What?" Julia asked. She scooted closer to me.

"I said, the bass is a little loud!"

"I can't hear you, the bass is too loud!" Julia yelled.

I pretended to take a sip of the beer in my plastic cup.

Marcella moved through the crowd, dancing with anyone she encountered.

"Excuse me," I said to Julia.

"What?"

"Never mind." I surged into the mass of sweaty teens in the living room. The furniture had been moved against the walls, leaving most of the space in the middle for dancing. I tugged on Marcella's arm. "Hey, is it all right if I turn the bass down?"

"What?" She was slithering down the front of some inebriated guy who apparently didn't even realize she was dancing with him.

"Can I turn the music down?"

She still couldn't hear me, but nodded anyway.

Pushing through the crowd, I found the CD player, and began fiddling with the dials. The bass finally stopped its relentless pounding, and I sighed in relief.

3

Fighting my way back to Julia, I spotted Aya and Hannah dancing by the fireplace.

"Hey!" I yelled.

They looked up and smiled. They lifted their drinks up over their heads, and danced their way over.

"Thank God someone turned the bass down." Aya took a sip of her drink. "It was giving me a headache."

Seconds later, the bass was cranked back up. I turned to look in the direction of the CD player. Marcella waved at me and gave me a thumbs up. Ugh.

Flash.

Bellevue Police Department.

Yes, my neighbors are out of town and it appears as though their daughter is having a very loud party. Can you send someone out?

Crap.

"Come on girls." I pulled my friends into the kitchen. "Dump your drinks out. Someone has called the police."

"How do you know that?" Hannah asked.

"I saw someone through the window just a little while ago. I think it was the neighbor," I said.

"How do you know they called the cops?" Aya dumped her beer in the sink and threw her cup in the garbage.

"I just have a feeling. Let's go." I dumped my full drink down the drain, and then herded them out the kitchen door.

We walked a block to my car.

"I definitely don't want to get caught drinking." Hannah twirled her hair nervously. "I'd be kicked off the basketball team."

"Maybe we should have warned everybody," Julia said, looking uncertainly back at the house.

"Most of those kids would've panicked and tried to drive home drunk. It's better this way." I felt slightly guilty for not telling anyone else at the party to leave. I hoped they didn't get into too much trouble.

"What about you?" Hannah asked, getting into the back seat.

"I didn't drink anything. My head hurts; and besides—I'm driving."

Minutes later, two cop cars drove by, headed toward Marcella's house. Sometimes my affliction worked to my advantage.

Chapter 2

The week flew by quickly. Every day was packed with classes, homework, and extra cheerleading practice. This weekend, we were playing Issaquah High School in the basketball championship game. It was a big deal.

On Friday morning, I got to school a little early to avoid the crowds. Ever since I was little, I'd had premonitions, but they were easy to ignore. Now they were becoming more frequent. It was getting harder and harder to pretend that I was normal. Having so many people around, hearing all their thoughts; it just drained the energy from me.

As I walked up the stairs, a girl brushed past me. Her mousy hair hung in her face, covering one eye. My breath caught in my chest. Searing pain ripped through the underside of my left arm between my elbow and wrist. I gasped and grabbed my arm, rubbing frantically, trying to erase the pain. The girl turned to look at me and then quickly looked down at the floor. She quickened her pace, increasing the distance between us.

She cuts.

I had an impression of some kind of abuse.

Flash.

Stepfather's footsteps outside the bedroom door. No! Please, no!

My heart hurt for her and I wondered if there was any way I could help. A boy walking toward me gave me a curious glance. Could he tell?

I made it to my AP American Lit class with plenty of time to review for the pop quiz I knew was coming. I was one of the first students in the classroom. Justin came in and sat behind me. He coughed once, and blew his nose into his tissue. He coughed again, and kept at it for at least a minute.

I turned around in my seat and looked at him. His face was an ashen gray, only pinking up when he coughed.

"You okay?"

"Yeah." He coughed some more. "Just a cold."

As I was studying him, a strange sensation came over me.

Lungs… filling up with fluid slowly.

My own breathing became difficult, like I was fighting for air.

I shook the feeling off and cleared my throat. I had to say something. I couldn't let this go on. How would I say this without him knowing about me?

"Justin," I said carefully, "listen to me. You've got to get to a doctor. I think you might have pneumonia."

He shook his head and coughed some more. "No, no, I'm pretty sure it's just a cold. I haven't been sick that long."

"No—promise me. That cough sounds really terrible. Go to the doctor and have it checked out," I insisted.

"What are you? My mother?" he coughed.

"Promise me," I demanded.

"Yeah, yeah, okay already!" he said, irritated with me.

"At least go to the school nurse," I said. "She'll be able to tell whether or not you need to see a doctor."

He glared at me. Just then, another round of coughs wracked his body.

When he stopped, I glared back at him.

7

"Go," I said.

He stood up and grabbed his pack off the back of his chair. "Fine," he muttered, "if it will make you happy."

He left the room as most of the other students sauntered into the classroom. Julia sat down in the desk next to mine.

"Where is Justin going?" she asked.

"I told him he should go see the school nurse," I said nonchalantly. "He had a nasty cough. I didn't want his sick germs all over me."

"Oh yeah, eeww. I hate it when people cough around me," she agreed, pulling her books out of her backpack and arranging them on the desk.

"Class," Ms. Reinhardt said. "Put your books away. We're having a pop quiz."

***

If I could just get through Anatomy and Physiology without anyone's issues overwhelming me, I could survive the day. I really wished I hadn't stood in the front though; I had a perfect view of the pig fetus laid out on the counter.

"The key thing here," said Mr. Foster, "is to cut through the layers of the abdominal wall so you can peel it back—without cutting the organs all up."

"Gross!" the girl to my left squealed. Nervous giggles and constant chattering drowned out the teacher's voice.

My shallow breathing pulled my mask in and out, the paper fabric scratching my lips.

"Lucky for us, these pig fetuses are rather young— much easier to cut into." His voice rose above the din. "Now you can open the last layer of tissue…"

His knife cut into the remaining skin and some kind of liquid spurted out, splashing onto my cheek. The medicinal smell was overpowering; my eyes teared up behind the goggles. My heart raced—my body shook uncontrollably.

The sounds of the students shrieking were replaced by the sound of my heart pounding like a drum. My vision clouded and the classroom melted away.

Flash.

Walking.

Footsteps behind me.

A hand, out of nowhere, clamped over my mouth—a damp cloth pressing into my nose and lips.

The smell... oh, the smell! I couldn't breathe. What was happening?

Blackness.

"Jenny?"

My eyes fluttered open.

Mr. Foster knelt beside me. I was lying on my back on the cold floor of the lab. A few girls hovered over me, snickering and hiding their smiles behind their gloved hands. Several boys inched forward and helped me to sit up.

"*That* was awesome!" said Chris Buehler as he pulled the goggles off my head.

"Yeah," said his stupid friend next to him, "I've never seen a chick faint before!"

I groaned and rubbed the back of my head. What had possessed me to take two freakin' science classes this year?

"All right, everyone, show's over," Mr. Foster said as he pushed the boys back. "Let's give Jenny a little breathing room. Some people get a little queasy during dissections—happens in this class every year."

I wished that were the only reason I had passed out. What *was* that? A premonition?

The teacher helped me up, patting me on the back. I reached for the countertop to steady myself.

"Nice goin', Jenny," Chris said as he elbowed me in the side. "Hope you don't do that at the basketball game tonight."

9

"Shut up," I mumbled.

"Chris!" Mr. Foster said sharply. "That's enough. Why don't you help Jenny to a chair at the back of the room while I finish up this demonstration?"

"Gladly!" Chris grinned and put his arm around my waist. His fingers moved a little farther up, inching closer to my chest.

He leaned in and whispered into my ear. "You are so hot."

My eyes narrowed and I wrenched myself away from his grip. I had a sudden urge to kick him in the balls, but I was still too shaky to do it. I found a seat near the back and plunked down, covering my face with my hands. Anything to keep that smell away.

***

"Oh my God!" Julia said as she caught up with me by the lockers. "I heard what happened in your science class today."

I sighed as I worked the combination lock. Juicy news always traveled fast in this school.

"Talk about embarrassing," I muttered.

Julia opened her locker and shoved in her over-stuffed backpack.

"So, what happened? The little oinkers made you sick?" She grinned as she slammed the metal door with a bang.

"I think it was the smell more than anything else," I said, remembering the feel of the hand over my mouth, the panic bubbling up in my chest. *No, don't think about it.*

"I'm sorry that happened to you—it must have been really humiliating."

I closed my locker door. "Hopefully, everyone will forget about it by the time the game starts tonight," I said as we headed down the hall toward the cafeteria.

10

"Doubtful," Julia giggled.

Aya and Hannah came down the hall toward us.

"I can't wait to see the game," Hannah was saying. But then she caught sight of Julia and me. "I heard about..."

"Hey!" Aya interrupted, pushing her out of the way. "I heard about you fainting in class!" Her dark eyes sparkled with amusement.

"Oh, for God's sake." I rolled my eyes. "Can't I just have my most embarrassing moment in private?"

She laughed, shaking her head. "If it was in private, then it wouldn't be your most embarrassing moment, would it?"

Thoughts of the images I had seen in class crept back into my mind. Something told me that the person who had pressed the cloth to my face in my vision had been a killer.

Chapter 3

The scoreboard ticked down the time remaining.

"Three, two, one," the crowd chanted.

By the time the clock hit one, the ball had left Blake's fingertips from center court and soared through the air. I held my breath. I watched as the ball sailed high across the gym in slow motion. Swooooosh! The crowd roared. My eardrums nearly exploded from the noise. The Pep Band struck up our fight song.

"We won!" Julia shouted, jumping up and down.

People rushed the court, surrounding the team members, hugging and whooping.

"Come on, girls, we're up," said Kassy, the head cheerleader.

We pushed our way onto the gym floor.

"Here they come!" shouted a boy in the crowd.

We pressed through the crowd and out into center court. It was time for our signature pyramid—I was ready to perform my spectacular mid-air flip off the top.

Kassy gave us the signal and our squad got into their positions. The second tier of girls climbed up to their posts. Laura, one of the cheerleaders at the base, gave me the go-ahead to climb up. She grunted as I climbed past her and added my weight to the girls perched on her back.

I made a note to myself to go light on the after-game pizza. I carefully ascended to the top of the groaning bodies.

Just as my right foot left the linked hands of the girls below me, I quickly kneeled and then stood on the quivering top of the pyramid. I steadied myself and then turned with my back to the left side of the risers. The crowd, suddenly silent, turned to watch.

My knees bounced once, twice, then a third time as I catapulted my body backward into my flip.

Flash.

White light.

Then darkness.

I heard a whimpering moan—was that coming from me? A sweaty, pale face hovered over mine. The man was grinning, a knife in his hand.

"Jenny! Jenny! Jenny?"

"Oh my God! Is she dead?"

The sounds of the gymnasium came back to me and then faded.

Gray… black… nothing.

*** *

My head hurt.

What was that beeping noise?

"Jenny?"

Was that Dad's voice? Why couldn't I open my eyes?

Mom's perfume. She had to be here somewhere.

My body felt as heavy as a rock.

"Can you hear us?"

Beep, beep, beep.

"I just saw her hand twitch. I think she's waking up."

The talking seemed a little louder. I sensed light behind my eyelids.

13

"She's definitely coming around."

I used every bit of energy I had to open my eyes.

"Jenny!" My mom patted my cheek. "Get the doctor, she's awake."

I opened my eyes a crack. I could barely make out the shape of my dad standing next to me, holding my hand.

"Jenny," my dad whispered at my side. "Are you okay? Do you know who I am?"

"Dad," I croaked.

"Oh, thank God! Mary, she's awake. She knows me!"

A doctor was standing at my right side with my mom positioned just behind him. He peered over me, his four faces swimming in front of me. Finally, he snapped into focus—his tired blue eyes watched me intently.

"Jenny, it's Dr. Williams. Do you know where you are?"

"Hospital?" I asked.

"Do you know what day it is?" he asked.

"Um, it's the day of the big game against Issaquah High. Uh, Friday, February 6th?"

"Yes, that's right. Good job. Do you remember the accident?" Dr. Williams asked as he began examining me.

I shook my head. "All I remember is standing at the top of the pyramid..." I suddenly remembered the creepy sweaty-faced guy hovering over me.

"Oh, wait, the guy with the knife!" I blurted out breathlessly.

My mom gave me a very worried look. "Knife?" she asked.

The doctor turned off the light he was shining in my eyes and peered at my mother, his eyebrows raised.

She stiffened and her face blanched.

"I must have dreamt it when I was out." I chewed on my lip. "No, all I remember is standing on top of the pyramid. Obviously, I must have fallen. Am I okay?" I asked.

14

"I think so. You have a concussion." Dr. Williams said.

"Oh. Is that all?" I attempted a smile.

My dad shook his head. "I can't believe she's able to joke around."

Mom squeezed Dad's arm.

"It's nothing to take too lightly," Dr. Williams said. "You really need to take it easy for a while. Does your head hurt?"

I swallowed hard. "Yeah. I feel a little foggy too."

"That's pretty standard for a concussion. We'll take a CT scan and an MRI. What about your stomach? Are you nauseous?"

My stomach rolled. I laid my hand on my belly and groaned.

The nurse pushed a bed pan toward me just as I threw up. It splattered up the sides, nearly escaping the rim of the bowl.

"Oh, Jenny!" My mom put her hand on my shoulder. "You poor thing!"

The doctor made some notes in his chart. "I'll get those tests ordered." He slipped out of the room.

"Sweetie, you sure scared us," my dad whispered. "That fall was worse than anything I've ever seen. I thought you were..." he said with tears in his eyes, the lines on his face etched deeper with worry.

I'd never seen my dad cry before. It scared me to see his raw emotion. I felt awful that I had caused my parents so much anxiety.

And what terrified *me* was the image of the man holding the knife. Who was he? Why did I see him at that particular moment? I wondered if this vision was related to the one I had in my science class.

A nurse came in.

"Mr. and Mrs. Crumb, I'm going to get Jenny set up for some tests. Why don't you go down to the cafeteria and get something to eat?" She smiled warmly and ushered my parents out of the room. They looked back at me reluctantly.

"Do we have to go?" my mom asked. "She just woke up. I'm not sure I want to leave her here by herself."

"She's not alone, Mrs. Crumb. Don't worry, she's in good hands with us. And besides, we need to get some work done. You'd just be bored sitting around in the waiting room."

"We love you, Jenny." She rushed back over to my side and hugged me fiercely.

"Come on, let's go see how bad hospital cafeteria food really is," Dad said as he scooted in and hugged me as well.

I listened to their footsteps disappear into the nighttime noises of the hospital.

"Okay, Jenny," the nurse said. "Why don't you rest for a few moments. We'll be back to get you set up for your CT scan in about fifteen minutes or so."

The fifteen minutes turned into at least thirty minutes. I closed my eyes for a moment, and my body succumbed to sleep.

The sweaty, pale-faced man hovered over me.

"Don't worry, you'll have everything you need here," he said in his high quavering voice.

"No, no, please don't leave me here. Please!" I begged.

"You'll be fine," he said. "I've left you some water; you should have enough air. Here's a blanket in case you get cold."

"No! Please! I'll be good, I'll be good!" I screamed.

"Don't worry, I've thought of everything. Here's a lamp. The battery should be okay for a while."

He closed the lid. I heard him crunching above and then the shovel flinging the dirt on top. The sounds became

*muffled as the dirt covered the roof. His footsteps clomped
away and then I was alone.*

The lamp flickered, and then went out.

"Noooooooo!!"

Two nurses ran into the room. I was sweating and
crying uncontrollably, my hands clawing at the non-
existent cell roof.

"Jenny!" One of the nurses came to my side, while the
other checked my vital signs.

"What happened? Did you fall out of bed? You were
screaming."

"I, I…" I sobbed.

The shorter blond nurse, who had been in my room
before, took my face in her hands. "Look at me," she said
calmly. "You are in the hospital. You're safe. I think you
probably just had a bad dream. That's it, isn't it? A bad
dream?" she asked.

"Yes." I hiccuped back another sob. But it wasn't a
dream, it was a vision.

She leaned me back down onto the soft pillow.

"Now take a deep breath."

I took a few shallow breaths.

She frowned and shook her head. "No, not like that—
deep breaths. She demonstrated by closing her eyes and
taking breaths through her nose. The fabric on her too-tight
uniform looked like it would split.

I made myself copy her and began to feel more
relaxed.

She nodded her approval.

"Yup, you've got it."

She gently sat me up and plumped up the pillow
behind me. She straightened the sheet and blanket over me.
The taller nurse took the cup sitting by the side of my bed
and left the room. She came back just a few seconds later
with the cup filled with ice water and a straw.

"Here you go, honey," she said. She brought the straw to my lips and I took a long deep sip. The cold water felt so good in my desert-dry throat.

"Thank you," I whispered.

The blond nurse smoothed the hair away from my face.

What did that dream mean? It was the same man I saw right before I fell off the pyramid. Was this guy out to get me? A wave of panic came over me. I took a deep breath to try and calm myself.

My heart raced, but I pushed away the thoughts and tried to think about something else.

"Let's get you in for your tests," the taller nurse said.

They wheeled my bed into the hall. I watched the ceiling lights go by. I almost hoped I had something seriously wrong with me. A brain tumor maybe? At least that would explain why my visions were getting more frequent and intense lately. If I was lucky, it wouldn't be cancerous, and they could just remove it. Then maybe I could live a normal life like everyone else.

Chapter 4

The test results were in. Aside from a concussion, nothing major was wrong with me. I had been lying around at home for a week now, bored out of my mind. Now that it was Sunday, I was so stir-crazy, I could hardly stand it. I wanted to go out with my friends, an idea my parents quickly shot down.

I sighed, and sat up in bed. Reaching over to my window, I opened my blinds. Morning light streamed in through the slats, and my room was bathed in sunshine. Surprisingly, February in Washington State could be pretty nice. There were a few days during the month that were actually sunny and warm. This was one of them.

I looked around my large bedroom with renewed appreciation. Out of all the rooms in our house, this was by far my favorite. When I was eleven years old, I begged my dad to paint it a very light rose petal pink. Now at seventeen, I still secretly loved it. To me, it was very reassuring and homey—just what I needed right now.

A light knock at my door startled me. It swung open, and my friends, Hannah, Aya, and Julia peeked around the edge of the door frame.

"Hi guys," I managed a smile. "Come on in."

Hannah walked over to the left side of the bed. She was the only one of us who wasn't a cheerleader—she played center for the girls' basketball team.

"Hey there. You look like crap!" she joked.

"Yeah, thanks a lot!" I made a feeble attempt to swipe at her.

She smirked. "God, you're so lame! You can't even hit me!"

Aya sat on my bed. "Hey, lay off, Hannah," she said with a wry smile. "Hasn't the poor girl been through enough without your incredibly bad sense of humor?"

Julia hung back a little bit. She looked worried.

"Are you okay?" she asked nervously. "I was so scared!"

She stood next to Hannah and took my hand.

"God, I'm so sorry! I feel so responsible! I mean, I was right below you, I should have tried to catch you!" The fingers on her right hand flew up to her long light brown hair, twirling it around.

"Julia, it wasn't your fault. You couldn't have kept me from hitting the floor. I don't remember what happened after I did the flip. I think I blacked out in mid-air or something."

"Maybe I could have cushioned your fall." Tears streamed down her cheeks. "I'm sorry."

Hannah and Aya exchanged an uneasy glance.

"Come on, Julia," Hannah said. "You heard Jenny, you couldn't have kept her from falling. Stuff like this happens sometimes."

Aya tugged on the string of her hoodie. "Yeah, I know it's not the first time something like this has happened. Just last year, a cheerleader from Mercer Island broke her arm after she fell off a pyramid, and she hadn't even done her jump off the top yet. I heard that she just slipped while climbing up to the second tier."

"That's what ya get for being a cheerleader," Hannah teased. "Sometimes you gotta pay the price."

Julia wiped her tears and she bit her lip to hide her smile. "You're just jealous. I think your secret dream is to be on the squad."

20

"Oh, please," snorted Hannah. "Then I'd have to wear ribbons in my hair, do my nails, and giggle all the time."

This time all three of us made a swipe at her.

"Hey!" She jumped out of the way. "Cut it out, you're going to ruin my hair and makeup."

It was just like Hannah to make jokes. I was glad for it though. Watching Julia cry was depressing.

"So, what's been going on in school since I've been gone? Any juicy gossip?" I asked.

"Oh my God," Aya said excitedly. "Caitlin and Josh are dating!"

"Seriously?" I asked. "They don't seem to be a good match."

"Yeah, I know! It won't last. Oh—and Sarah dumped James."

I grinned. "Well, we all saw that one coming, didn't we?"

"Oh, and one more thing," Hannah said, her tone turning more serious.

"What?" I asked.

"Well, you know Callie Shoemaker?" Hannah asked.

"Callie… sophomore? The girl who is in all the school plays?" I asked.

"Yeah, that's her," Hannah continued. "Well, she's missing."

"Missing?" I asked. "You mean, like, she's skipping school or something? Or ran off with her boyfriend?"

"No," said Aya, shaking her head. "Callie doesn't have a boyfriend. We mean, missing… like she didn't show up for school. No one has seen her since."

My skin crawled. "Whoa," I let that sink in for a few seconds. "When did this happen?"

"Last Friday," said Julia.

"Well, I hope they find her soon," I said. "I hope she's okay."

My friends nodded in agreement.

21

Dad appeared in the doorway with a tray of orange juice and scones. "You ladies interested in some breakfast?"

"Oh my God, yes!" Hannah did a fist-pump, eyeing the tray.

Dad set it down on the floor, and my friends converged upon the food like a bunch of vultures.

"Leave some for Jenny!" Dad chuckled and headed back down the stairs.

Aya handed me a glass of juice and a scone. "Don't get crumbs in your bed."

"I'll try not to." I took a bite of the pumpkin scone and savored the spicy deliciousness.

The chatter stopped while we munched. Soon all that was left was a few crumbs and some empty glasses with orange pulp stuck to the rims.

I yawned and leaned back down on my pile of pillows.

"We should probably let Jenny get some rest," Hannah said.

"Oh, you don't have to go," I said. "You guys just got here." My eyelids drooped, and I stifled another yawn.

"No, we should definitely let you sleep," Aya said as she got up off the floor.

Julia gathered up the dishes, and piled them onto the tray. "Will you be in school on Monday?"

"I think so. I'll see what my mom and dad think."

"Okay, but don't push it," Hannah said.

My friends hugged me and left the room quietly. Amazing that these girls had known me since I was four years old; they knew everything about me. But they didn't *really* know who I was.

I closed my eyes. I would just rest for a few moments before taking a shower.

It was dark and cold. I was trembling.

Crunch, crunch, crunch.

Footsteps... above me.

The feeling of dread crept through my veins, sending a chill down my spine. I held my breath in the underground box, waiting for the lid to be uncovered and air to spill into my dank prison.

I gasped for air. What the hell? I must have fallen asleep. Sitting up in bed, I ran my fingers through my hair. This was what, the fourth time I'd had a dream like this? First the cloth over my nose, then the guy with the knife, and the last two about being buried in an underground cell.

My body shook. I needed to get into the shower. Maybe the water would wash these visions away.

***

After my shower, I felt much better. I was able to do more than just lie around in bed. I spent most of the afternoon reading Facebook posts, watching YouTube videos, and texting my friends. I almost felt like myself again.

"Jenny! Dinner!" my mom called from downstairs. My stomach rumbled. It was only 4:00 p.m., but I guess I was kind of hungry.

Carefully, I walked downstairs, holding onto the handrails.

Mom had made my favorite dinner: grilled chicken, pesto pasta, and a big salad.

"Why such an early dinner?" I asked.

"We are celebrating." Mom tossed the salad and set the bowl in the middle of the table.

As we sat down to eat, my little brother, Jackson, wrinkled up his nose. "Ewww! Yuck! Why couldn't we have hamburgers instead? I hate pesto!" he whined.

Mom gave him a stern look. "In case you hadn't noticed, your sister has had a serious injury. This is the least we can do to make her feel better, don't you think?"

My brother was ten years old, but you'd think he was three, given his taste in food. His favorites were hamburgers, fries, macaroni and cheese, grilled cheese sandwiches, and cheese pizza. I was sure his arteries were already clogged up with congealed goo.

"Grow up, Jackson," I said. "Your taste buds are so immature."

"Yeah, well your *brain* is immature," he said making a face at me.

I rolled my eyes. "Whatever."

My dad grimaced. "Cut it out, you guys, this is supposed to be a nice family dinner. We don't need all this bickering. And Jackson, give your sister a break. She's had a rough week. Correction—we've *all* had a rough week."

"Not me!" chirped Jackson. "I got to have a sleepover while you guys were at the hospital. And she's been holed up in her room for a week. I finally had some peace and quiet from her big mouth!"

Dad put his hand on Jackson's shoulder. "I said— enough!"

The tone of voice made Jackson sober up a bit. He ate a bite of pasta and scowled as he chewed. Dad gave him a look that made the scowl fade away.

I took a bite of my pasta. "Mmmmmm...." I said dreamily. "This has got to be the best pesto you have ever made, Mom!"

"Thanks, sweetie." She leaned over and kissed my cheek. "I'm so glad you're okay!"

I gave her a light hug and then dug into my dinner.

My dad cleared his throat. "Have you given any thought as to what kind of after school activity you want to do?

"Huh?" I took a sip of my water. "What do you mean?"

"You know, the doctor said you might want to lay off cheerleading for a couple of months or even the rest of the year. You need to avoid any further injuries to your head."

"But just for a little while, right? I don't think I need a couple of months or certainly not the rest of the year to recover."

Mom's face tightened. "Jenny, I think it would be best if you *did* take the rest of the year off. Maybe you should take up a different extra-curricular activity. Something like the yearbook committee or theatre?"

"How 'bout chess?" my dad joked. "That's about as safe an activity as I can think of."

"Yes, and probably the most boring activity I can think of." I hesitated. "I really like cheerleading a lot—a whole lot. And I'm really good at it." I was starting to feel panicked. Cheerleading was the one thing that kept me feeling somewhat normal and grounded—like I was a part of something mainstream. They couldn't take that away from me. But if I fought them right now, they would dig in and I'd lose this battle. It was best to let some time go by. In a few weeks, when my injuries were gone, they would let down their guard, and I could probably go back to it without a fight.

"Well, take a little time to think about it," my mom said, chewing her bottom lip.

"I will."

Chapter 5

"Are you sure you want to go back to school?" Mom set a cup of tea and a plate of cinnamon toast down in front of me. It was 6:00 in the morning. I was dressed and ready to go even though school didn't start until 7:30.

"Yes, Mom! I'm ready. I'm so tired of being locked up in my room. I need to get out of the house."

"Well, if that's what it is, I can take the day off of work, and we can go shopping," Mom said hopefully.

I shook my head. "I really don't want to fall behind in school. I've already lost a week—it's going to be tough enough to get back up to speed."

Her shoulders slumped. "Oh, okay… if you really think you can handle it."

"Yes, I can do this." I got up from the table, and put my dishes on the counter. "Will you drive me?"

"Sure," Mom answered. "I'm definitely not okay with you driving yourself."

To be honest, I wasn't okay with that either. The thought of driving scared me to death. What if I had another vision? I could crash. I didn't want to hurt myself or anyone else for that matter.

***

26

"Good morning, students!" Mr. Fletcher, our principal, said into the microphone. We sat on the bleachers in the gym. No one bothered to respond; most kids didn't actually wake up until at least 10:00 a.m.

"I'd like to introduce you to our special guest, Roy Landau, from an organization called Leaders of the 21st Century."

About half the crowd clapped unenthusiastically. Assemblies were not our favorite thing, but most students were glad to get out of class.

Roy stepped up to the podium and cleared his throat. "Good morning! I'm so happy to be here at Newport High School today!"

A smattering of applause sounded in the large gym. At least there were a couple of enthusiastic hoots when he mentioned our school name.

"Being a leader is more important today than in any other time period to date," he said. "And you are probably wondering why."

"Not really," Aya muttered beside me.

"I'll tell you why. There has never been a time in our history where there is so much competition. We no longer live in a world where we compete just with our immediate community members. America is competing in a global economy. If you don't have leadership skills, you will be left behind."

Julia inspected her nails. "I don't even know what he's talking about."

"Today is going to be all about teamwork. Because to be a good leader," the man continued, "you have to trust your team."

Hannah pulled her cell phone out of her pocket and started texting someone.

"When you are a leader, you are invariably going to be working with a team in some capacity. You'll need to

27

draw on team synergy, and know when to lead, and when to follow. Trust is key."

"Oh my God, I'd almost rather be in class right now," Julia huffed.

"So, now I want you to come down off the bleachers and break into groups of ten or so people."

Nobody moved.

Mr. Fletcher stepped up to the microphone. "Come on down, students."

Reluctantly, people stood up and shuffled onto the gym floor. Teachers helped break the students into groups.

I found myself in a group with Julia and eight other people I barely recognized.

"We're going to play an icebreaker game first," Roy said. "Each group will be given a beach ball. The person who starts will say, 'My name is Roy—or whatever their first name is. Then they will throw the ball to someone in the group. Then the person who catches it says, 'Thank you, Roy. My name is John or whatever.' This is a quick way to learn each other's names before we start the other exercises."

The teachers and staff began passing beach balls out to all the groups. Soon, we were passing the ball around and learning each other's names.

"Next, I want you to go around the circle and say the name of a leader that you admire and why," Roy said. "For example, if I said I admire Abraham Lincoln, I could also say that I admire him because he was responsible for ending slavery in our country."

We went around the circle, and finished quickly. I said I admired Gandhi because of his commitment to peace and non-violence. But I was shocked by some of the answers in my group. One girl said, "Mickey Mouse." Apparently, she found this incredibly funny, and she broke into a fit of giggles. O...kay.

Next came a series of similar exercises, followed by the grand finale, the trust game.

"A good leader has to take risks at times. And risk is all about trust. You can't take risks unless you trust that a good outcome is possible. To do that, you need to trust your team. I want one person to volunteer to stand in the middle of your circle."

Julia snorted, and I felt her hands on my back. Suddenly, I was standing in the middle of the circle. Crap. I shook my head. "No, I don't want to do this."

"Sure you do!" she laughed. "Come on, it'll be fun."

"Now," Roy said, "I want the person in the middle to close their eyes tightly—no peeking."

Why did Julia do this to me?

"Close your eyes," she insisted.

"Then, one person from the group steps forward and gently spins the person around, and then leads them to a person in the group. The middle person then has to lean or fall backward while the first person catches them. The middle person has to have their backs to the person catching them."

I sucked in a breath. I didn't like this idea at all.

"Then that person passes the middle person to the next person in the circle, until everyone has caught the middle person."

Mom was right. I should have waited one more day before returning to school.

Julia giggled. "Close your eyes."

She began spinning me. I didn't think this was a very good idea, given that I had just suffered a concussion. But if I said something now, people might think that I was just chicken.

The spinning stopped, and she led me to someone, and turned my back to them. I was dizzy, and my heart was pounding.

"Okay, lean back," she said.

I felt disoriented. What if the person didn't catch me?

She shoved me backward, and I lost my balance. Arms caught me.

Flash.

This might be the only time I get to hold a hot blonde. I wish I were alone with her.

Yuck.

He passed me to the next person. Julia shoved me backward again.

Flash.

Oh, man, I'm so hungry. I should've eaten breakfast this morning.

The next person.

Flash.

I forgot to do my Algebra homework! But it's after lunch period, so maybe I'll just skip lunch and do it then.

On to the next.

Flash.

"That's a cute outfit. I wonder where she got it."

Next.

Flash.

I hope I covered up the bruise enough. My dad would really lose it if someone reported this to the school.

Oh no. I couldn't handle this much longer.

Next.

Flash.

No one likes me. Even Mom said she wished I'd never been born.

I broke out into a cold sweat.

Flash.

Oh, the stuff I could do to her. Look at those tits...

My stomach churned. This was too much.

Julia's turn.

Flash.

This looks like fun. I don't know why Jenny didn't want to do it. She's acting all weird. She's actually sweating. What's up with…

"Okay, let's stop here, guys," Roy said.

I blew out a breath of relief, and opened my eyes. Everyone was staring at me. I wiped the sweat off my forehead.

"Jenny, are you okay?" Julia asked.

I swallowed. "Um, yeah."

Julia looked horrified. "Oh my God! I'm so sorry. I didn't even think about your concussion!"

I blinked numbly.

"Why don't you all take your seats again," Roy suggested. "We're going to watch a fun movie about how great leadership can shape our future world."

***

I barely made it through the rest of the day. The trust exercise had completely thrown me for a loop. My first day back at school had left me feeling scared and exhausted. How much longer could I go on like this? Every year the visions became more powerful, and more frequent. I had a fleeting fantasy about becoming a hermit and living in a cave on a high mountaintop.

I sighed and watched my mom's black SUV pull up to the curb.

"How was your day?"

"Okay, I guess." I shifted the backpack in my lap.

"What does that mean?" Mom pulled out of the parking lot, and drove to the first stoplight. "Did you get dizzy, or feel sick?"

The light had turned red, and she turned to look at me expectantly.

"No, nothing like that happened."

31

"Then what?" The light turned green, and her eyes turned back to the road.

"I guess I'm just tired. Maybe I just need to rest."

"That's an excellent idea."

We drove in silence for a few minutes. Rain began to fall lightly onto the windshield. The wipers swished on and off. We pulled into our driveway, and Mom pushed the remote to open the garage. "Jenny, is anything else wrong? I feel like there is something you're not telling me."

"No. That's all. I'm just tired. Really." I hurried out of the car, and shut the door. "Want to watch a movie with me?"

"Sure." The answer seemed to satisfy her. She opened the door to the kitchen. "Just for a little while, though. I need to make dinner."

After watching a movie and having a nice meal, I changed into cozy pajamas, and read my history textbook for the next day's quiz. I only read for fifteen minutes before my eyes became heavy with sleep. I clicked off the light, and let my book fall to the floor beside my bed.

At exactly 3:00 a.m., my eyes popped open. The green numbers from my digital alarm clock glowed eerily in the dark. The house was silent. Something felt different. I turned my head slightly to one side and saw something out of the corner of my eye.

Chapter 6

My heart ka-thumped in my rib cage, my hands were instantly sweaty. The air was charged with electricity. Someone was in my room and was watching me.

"Jenny."

I quickly rolled over onto my back and nearly screamed. I caught a flash of white... a ghost? No, something else. The image faded as quickly as it appeared.

"Jenny."

Holy crap. What the hell was going on? I scanned the room frantically, looking for any glimmer of light or movement.

"I know you can hear me."

I sat up and sucked in my breath. Before I could scream, the voice said, *"Do not be afraid."*

Afraid? Afraid was a gross understatement.

I must be crazy.

"Who are you? *What* are you?" I stammered.

"You were born with a gift," the female voice said. *"A gift that you've tried to deny up until now. I'm here to tell you that you need to accept the gift. Life will be very different for you now. It will frighten you, but it is important that you use the gift that God gave you."*

This had to be a dream. A really weird dream.

"What gift? I don't know what you are talking about."

"I think you do know," she answered. *"You see things, you know things..."*

I can't," I said, shaking my head. "I don't want the gift..."

"Most people who have it don't want the gift at first. You are not alone in that. Please learn how to use your ability—use it to help people."

"How?" I whispered incredulously. "How do I use it?"

Why was I talking to this... person... or whatever? This was just a dream.

"This is your own journey, you must find out on your own," she said.

"What?" I asked incredulously. "How?"

"You will know."

Hands down, this was the craziest dream yet.

"You need to trust in yourself," she said reassuringly. I saw another flash of white before she faded into the darkness. A white feather drifted down toward my bed. Holding my hand out, I caught it in my palm. I stared at it in awe.

"Wait!" I called. "Wait! What do you mean that life will be very different? What am I supposed to do?"

She was gone. My words echoed faintly in the dark room.

I swung my legs out of bed and got up, feeling my way to the bathroom. I turned on the light and filled my cup with cold water, my hands shaking. Weird.

Dream, Jenny. That was just a dream, I thought as I took a sip.

Seriously? Was it a dream or was that for real? My heart still pounded in my ears.

I looked at myself in the mirror. It was just me. I didn't look any different than I had before. It had to be a dream. I ran the water again, splashing it on my face. I wanted very much for this to not be real.

I went quietly back to bed and slipped under the covers.

I lay awake thinking. Was I going insane? This whole thing was unbelievable. But strangely enough, I was starting to think that this person might be an angel. Even if I did believe in angels, which I wasn't sure that I did, why would one show up in my bedroom? Just to give me a message? From all accounts that I'd ever heard, angels showed up to save people who were in dire situations or accidents. And maybe the people who told those stories were crazy anyway.

I thought about the reality of this vision or dream and finally gave up. I closed my eyes and forced myself to relax.

Crunch, crunch, crunch. Oh, God! He's back!

It was pitch black... and cold. The earthy smell of my surroundings nearly suffocated me. I heard some scuffling above, and dirt being scraped off the roof. And then a creak as daylight spilled into my cell. The fresh air felt inexplicably good on my upturned face.

The sweaty-faced man peeked over the lid.

He smiled a crazy, unsettling smile. "Ah, you're still alive then! Good, good. I brought you some food."

He handed me a cooler and I lifted it eagerly to the side of my narrow cot, my stomach twisting with hunger and fear.

I awoke with a start. My heart was pounding.

"Just another weird dream," I mumbled to myself. Who was this man? I felt sure he was coming to get me. Is that why I was dreaming about him again? And then I thought about my death premonition; the one about Grandpa Al.

I had a dream about him when I was four. In the dream, my grandfather was getting all of his fishing gear together. He was whistling as he packed the back of his car with a tackle box, fishing pole, and a cooler full of snacks.

The dream seemed so real. I could hear the birds singing, the breeze gently tickling my cheek…

Grandpa was on his way back into the garage to get the last of the gear. I waved at him, but he didn't see me. Suddenly, he grimaced and grabbed his left arm with his right hand. On his face, I could see that he realized what was happening. He fell to his knees and then thudded to the pavement. In that moment, I knew that he had died. My heart was filled with sadness.

When I woke up the next morning, I asked my mom if Grandpa Al was dead. She looked horrified.

"What? No, Grandpa Al is fine! Why would you say such a thing?"

I saw the look on her face… I could tell that I had upset her.

I answered, "I had a nightmare." I told her about how he was getting ready for his fishing trip and how I saw him fall to his knees holding his arm.

My mom looked relieved. "Oh, a nightmare," she said. "Honey, it was just a dream. People have bad dreams all the time. They don't really mean anything."

But she was wrong about that.

About two days later, the phone rang and it was my Grandma telling my mom that her husband of over thirty-five years had died of a sudden heart attack. My mom stared at me with a funny look on her face as tears streaked her cheeks. She was scared of me.

"Mom," she said quietly into the phone, "How did Dad die?"

She listened and looked at me again. Her face went from pale to white.

"Going fishing?" she mumbled, sinking down into the kitchen chair.

After she hung up the phone, she told me, "It happened just the way you described. I can't believe it. How did you know, Jenny?"

36

Her eyes were wide with fear. "How did you know?"

Shaking my head, I answered truthfully. "I told you. I saw it in my dream."

"I should've called my dad—I should have warned him!" She covered her face with her hands and cried harder.

Even at four years old, I somehow felt responsible. And I knew then that if I had another one of those dreams, I would be sure not to tell her. I didn't want her to be afraid of me. Maybe my dream had caused him to die…

I hadn't had one of those dreams in a long time.

There was a light knock on the door.

"Jenny?" My mom turned the knob and peeked in. "Are you all right? You look a little flushed." She put her hand on my forehead.

"I think I had kind of a scary dream, that's all," I said casually.

"A nightmare? Do you remember it?" Her face tightened.

"No," I lied.

"Well, I don't think you have a fever," she said as she felt my forehead. "How do you feel?"

"I'm fine."

"Good!" she said, looking relieved. "Why don't you get a shower and come down for breakfast. I made your favorite—hash browns and eggs, extra ketchup, and toast with strawberry jam."

"I'll shower fast." I rushed off to the bathroom.

***

After school, I needed to be alone. As usual, the energy from all those students had completely drained me. Getting some fresh air would be rejuvenating, and having time alone would help me to recharge.

"Mom, I think I'll go for a walk—get my circulation going again."

She furrowed her brows, looking anxious. "Are you sure, Jenny? You've only been home for a week. Don't you want to rest?"

"Mom! I've been resting for too long. Please ... the walk will do me good."

"How 'bout if I go with you?" she suggested nervously.

"Thanks for offering, but I really want to go out by myself. Is that okay?"

She thought for a moment and then agreed. "Don't go too far, please. And—take your cell phone."

"Thanks, Mom."

I grabbed my phone off the kitchen counter and let the door close quietly behind me. I knew exactly where I was headed. I walked briskly down my block and took a right at the next street.

A few rhododendron bushes were in bloom along the sidewalk, their bright red blossoms rustling gently in the breeze. I'd read somewhere that in the Pacific Northwest there were so many varieties of rhododendrons that every month of the year there was at least one variety that bloomed. I slowed my pace a bit as I rounded the corner, feeling the sun on my face. I zipped up my thick gray hoodie. Even though the sun was out, it was still chilly.

I walked another two blocks and entered the park. Despite the nice weather, there were no other people there today. I walked past the playground equipment and veered off to my favorite spot. Behind a straggling grove of cedar trees, a big light gray rock stood, lodged firmly into the ground. It was about six feet tall and maybe another ten feet wide. I climbed up to the top and sat down, closed my eyes, and sighed.

This had been my favorite place to think ever since we moved to this neighborhood. It was a favorite place for other kids to climb and jump off of too. At times, I had come here only to find a group of rambunctious boys climbing, pushing, and jumping off the rock, playing king of the mountain. During those times, I would go sit on one of the swings and wait. After a while, the boys got tired of their testosterone contest and would run off to find something or someone else to annoy. That's when I would get up and climb the rock to find peace.

I sat for a few minutes with my eyes closed, just breathing and smelling the air. Today there was the smell of cedar and something else that I couldn't identify. I opened my eyes to see what it was.

Flash.

The lid was open, I saw the sky. It was so beautiful! I could taste the sweetness of the air, but it was soon overpowered by a sickening smell—like a laboratory or rubbing alcohol? Chloroform or ether maybe?

His grin appeared over the lid, blocking the sun's rays.

"You didn't think I'd forgotten you, did you?" he sneered. "I'm having so much fun with you, I'm not sure I want to leave the ransom note ... I can't decide. Maybe I'll keep you a while longer. His hand reached out toward my face. In it was a white cloth saturated with the overpowering medicinal smell.

I gasped for air. I was back on my rock, suddenly sick to my stomach. I lurched off and threw up in the bushes.

God, what was happening to me? Maybe I truly was going crazy. I wiped my mouth with my sleeve and gingerly stood up, bending over with my hands on the rock.

"Are you okay?" a voice from behind me said.

I jumped and let out a squeak.

I turned around quickly, still holding on to the rock.

It was a girl I recognized from school, Madeline Coalfield.

"I'm sorry!" she said grabbing my arm to steady me. "I didn't mean to startle you!"

My heart was racing a mile a minute and I was breathing far too quickly for comfort.

"Here," she said, leaning me against the rock. "Try to rest a little."

"Thanks," I stumbled over the word. "I'm sorry. I don't usually barf in public."

"That's okay, I hear the flu is going around," she said, stepping back.

"Oh—no, I don't have the flu," I reassured her. "I think it was something I ate this morning. I don't have a fever." I put the back of my hand up to my forehead. "See? You can feel for yourself if you like." I gestured to her.

"No, that's okay. I believe you," she said with a little smile.

I studied her face. She was quite a pretty girl; blond, like me, but even more petite. She was maybe five foot three inches or so with beautiful light bluish-green eyes and a creamy pale complexion.

"You're a sophomore, right?" I asked.

"Uh huh."

I remembered now where I had seen her before, aside from walking past her in the hallways. She was in one of the recent school plays, playing the princess in *Once Upon a Mattress*.

She was silent for a moment and then said, "I'm glad you are okay… I mean, after your accident."

"Thanks," I said.

"Are you feeling all right?" she asked, looking more closely at me.

"Yeah, I'm fine."

"Do you want me to call anyone for you?" she asked pulling her cell phone out of her pocket. "Your parents, maybe?"

I shook my head, "No, I'm fine, really I am. I just live a couple of blocks away."

"Oh, I didn't know you lived so close! I live one block away from the park, on 60th."

"We're practically neighbors!" I glanced up the street, and shifted my feet.

"How 'bout if I walk you back home?" she asked, taking my arm.

The minute she touched my arm, I had a flash. In rapid succession, I saw images.

Five years old, learning how to ride a bike without training wheels.

Her mom congratulating her on a good report card.

Her dad coming home from work in his police car.

Playing cards with her mom, dad, and brother on the floor of their family room.

Auditioning for plays.

Friends from the theatre.

Callie Shoemaker. The missing girl?

"Jenny?" she shook my arm gently.

"Huh? Oh, sorry. I just spaced out for a second." I looked down at my shoes, embarrassed. I hope she didn't think I was weird.

"That does it. I'm walking you home," Madeline said with determination.

I shrugged.

We left the park and started walking back toward my house.

"Can I ask you something?" I said, stopping on the curb.

"Sure," she shrugged.

"Are you friends with Callie Shoemaker?" Why was I asking her this?

"Yes." Her shoulders sagged.

"Have they found her yet?"

She shook her head. "No."

41

"I'm so sorry," I said.

"She's my best friend. My life has pretty much turned upside down since she disappeared," she said quietly.

"Wow," I said as we stepped off the curb. "Do you have any idea where she might be? Do you think that she ran away?"

Madeline shook her head. "She would never, ever run away. Callie is a happy person. She had no reason to run away. I think something really bad must have happened to her."

We walked in silence the rest of the way to my house.

"Well, here we are," I said. "Thank you for making sure I got home all right. I really appreciate it."

"Anytime. See you at school." Madeline turned and walked back down the block. I watched as she rounded the corner and was out of sight.

I felt so sorry for her. If it were me, I would be going crazy trying to figure out what to do to help find my friend. There was something gnawing at the back of my brain, but I just couldn't get it to come to the surface.

Chapter 7

The next morning, I was feeling much more like myself—like I almost had my old life back. I wasn't dizzy or tired. I opened the car door.

"Mom? Can you pick me up after cheerleading practice?"

She looked at me funny. "I thought you were going to lay off of that for now. Remember? Doctor's orders."

"Actually, I think he just meant that I shouldn't do a flip off of the top of a pyramid…"

"No, I remember quite clearly," Mom said sternly. "You should lay off the cheerleading for a while."

"How 'bout if I just go watch? I'll only join in the floor stuff if there isn't much jumping around."

"Watching is fine," she said. "I think that's all you should do. Promise?"

"Okay," I said reluctantly. "I promise." She didn't see that I had my fingers crossed behind my back.

I got out of the car and slung my backpack over my shoulder.

Although it was warm, a cold breeze suddenly drifted past me, making the hair on the back of my neck prickle. I shivered and zipped my hoodie up a little higher.

There it was again. Had someone just brushed past me? I stopped and looked from side to side. Nothing.

"Hey, Jenny!"

I turned and saw Julia and Aya waving from the sidewalk near the front doors.

"Hey!" I yelled back.

They dashed over and hugged me.

"You are looking good this morning." Aya squeezed me tightly.

"Easy, Aya. You'll hurt her." Julia pulled her off of me.

"I am feeling great this morning. It's almost like I never got hurt."

We chattered non-stop all the way to the front door and through the commons and the hallways. I felt alive. This was going to be a great day. All of a sudden, I was noticing things that I had never really noticed before; the trophy case and the pictures of the ASB officers hanging in the hall. My eyes were drawn to a poster on the wall. MISSING. Below the title was a picture of Callie Shoemaker.

I bit my lip and stopped to stare at it.

"Jenny?" Julia tugged on my arm. "Come on, we'll be late to class."

***

The day went by quickly. The last bell of the day rang and I rearranged my stuff, switching things out of my backpack and putting unneeded books in my locker. Aya and Julia met me in the hallway and we walked toward the gym for cheerleading practice.

"I thought you weren't supposed to do cheerleading for a while," Julia said.

"Well, I told my mom that I was just going to watch," I said. "I might join in a little if you guys aren't working on flips or pyramids."

"Just don't overdo it," Aya said.

"Ugh! You sound like my mom!"

44

Aya smirked. "Gee, thanks."

As we walked into the gym, the other cheerleaders bounced over to me, hugging me and asking questions.

"How are you?"

"So glad you're back!"

"Can you still do flips?"

Our coach, Mrs. Bauder, saw me and silenced everyone. "Girls! That's enough! Leave poor Jenny alone, for heaven's sake! Everyone, go change; we only have an hour and a half to practice," she reminded them. "Jenny, can I talk to you for a second?"

"Sure." I shrugged.

She pulled me aside. "Can you participate today?"

"A little—as long as I don't over-exert myself or do anything too physical, I should be all right."

I felt a twinge of remorse as I lied to the coach, but the excitement of returning to my old life overpowered my conscience.

"You're sure?"

"Yup," I said, also feeling slightly guilty about promising my mom.

I changed into my capri sweats and t-shirt. The other girls had already changed and were out on the gym floor. I was thrilled to get back to practice. It felt like it had been forever since I had been working up a sweat and learning the dance and cheer routines.

Coach Bauder had us stretch and warm up for the first five to ten minutes, which felt great to me. But when she turned on the music and had us work on our floor routines, I started to feel a little nauseous and my head began to ache. I ignored it and kept working.

The next part of the routine involved cartwheels, which I stupidly tried.

Wham! Suddenly, I found myself lying flat on my back, pain ripping through my head. The music stopped

45

and eleven girls and one coach were staring down at me in a circle.

"Jenny?" Coach Bauder asked nervously. "Are you all right?"

"Uhhhooooohhhhh," I managed to groan.

Coach Bauder pushed the other girls aside. "Give her some air, please!"

The girls stepped back a little, looking worried.

"Julia! Go get the school nurse!" Coach Bauder barked.

Fifteen minutes later, I was sitting in the nurse's office, feeling very foolish. The room was small and starkly white. Hanging on the wall was a blood pressure cuff, a medical waste dispenser, and a Plexiglas holder containing a box of disposable latex gloves. I felt a little claustrophobic and panicked at the impending reaction of my mom. What was I going to say to her?

"I've called your mother," the nurse was saying to me. "She's on her way. You know, you shouldn't have tried the cartwheel. You are lucky that you only fell on your back, not your head."

"I know, I know," I mumbled.

Julia and Aya were in the nurse's office as well, jammed together, leaning against the only wall space in the room.

"Your mom is going to be so mad." Aya said.

"Yes, no need to remind me," I said.

"Yeah," Julia said. "She told you not to do cheerleading for a while. She will *not* be happy."

"Thanks so much for your words of encouragement," I grumbled. Geez. I knew what I had done was stupid, but did they have to rub it in?

Aya and Julia shrugged.

Just then, my mom rushed in and hugged me. "Oh my God, Jenny! Is she all right?" she asked, turning to the nurse.

"She's okay," the nurse said sternly. "But she really shouldn't be jumping around or doing cartwheels. That's just not safe right now."

"What? Where were you doing cartwheels?"

"Cheerleading practice," I mumbled, looking down at my hands.

"What? You said you would just *watch* cheerleading practice. I made you promise not to do anything but watch." She looked at me incredulously.

I looked down at my feet. "I'm really, really, really sorry," I said. "I just wanted for life to get back to normal again." I looked up at my mom.

"And you thought that by jumping around... that you could somehow make your life normal again? You could have re-injured yourself and ended up back in the hospital. Jenny, what were you thinking? My God! You could have died!" she raged.

Aya looked at Julia and then grabbed her hand. "Come on Julia, we better get back to practice."

"Good luck, Jenny," Julia said looking back as she and Aya went through the door. "Looks like you're going to need it."

Ugh. This sucked.

"Sorry," I said again to my mom.

"Sorry?" she repeated. "Is that all you can say? Oh no, Jennifer Rose, you can't dismiss this with a simple sorry."

Oh boy, now I'd done it. When my mom got riled up about something, she couldn't stop.

"No—let me lay down the rules for you, okay?" she continued, gesturing wildly with her hands. "You will not be returning to cheerleading this year. You will be lucky to EVER return to cheerleading. Do you understand?"

I nodded glumly.

"Furthermore, you will not go to cheerleading practice to even 'watch' as you so put it. You will either come straight home from school every day or you will find a *safe*

47

after-school activity that doesn't involve jumping, cartwheeling, or flinging yourself off of a stack of girls. Got it?"

"I understand," I muttered.

"I'm sorry, I didn't hear you," she said, her eyes sparking dangerously.

"Yes, Mom. No cheerleading." I sighed.

"You're damn right—no cheerleading," she puffed. Now that some of her anger was spent, she took it down a notch.

"Can you stand up?" she asked, taking my arm.

"Yes."

"Come on then," she urged. "We're going home."

She led me gently to the door. The nurse smiled at my mother approvingly. "Thank you, Ms. Donald," my mom said.

We left the school. It was a long and silent drive home.

Chapter 8

The next day, Mom was still stewing over my cartwheel debacle. I felt terrible. Why had I done it? It was dumb. Just plain old dumb. But still, I really *did* want everything to go back the way it was before the day of the big game. I realized that it probably wouldn't happen the way I wanted it to.

She dropped me off at school early because she had a meeting at work.

Since I had plenty of time to kill, I headed toward the girls' bathroom. The halls were empty, except for a girl walking slowly down the hall. She was dressed in retro clothes; flared or bell-bottom jeans and an orange t-shirt. Her long brown hair was braided in pig-tails. Her pretty face was lined with worry and sadness. She stopped when she saw me.

"Have you seen my boyfriend?" she asked. "I can't find him."

"No," I shook my head. "Who is your boyfriend?"

"John Cook. He's a senior," she said.

"A senior? Are you sure?" I asked.

"Of course, I'm sure."

"That's funny," I said. "I'm a junior and I know just about all of the seniors. I've never seen or heard of him. Is he new here?"

She shook her head, "No, he's been at this school since freshman year."

She walked sadly past me.

I turned around to ask her to describe him to me, but she was gone. I mean gone, gone. Not walking away or turning a corner or anything like that. She was just plain gone. All the hairs on the back of my neck stood up. That was pretty creepy.

Was she a ghost or just a weird girl who could move at the speed of light?

I sighed. As if all this other stuff wasn't bad enough, now I was seeing ghosts too.

When the last bell finally rang, I was exhausted. My mom had asked me to catch the bus home because she had an appointment. On my way out the door, I passed by the gym. I couldn't resist peeking through the glass windows in the door. There was another cheerleading practice going on. I caught a glimpse of my friends. There was a new girl in there too. She was pretty, with long streaked dark hair and olive skin. Marcella Jackson. She had been waiting for this moment for a long time. I watched her flicking her pom-poms like a pro. As much as I didn't like her, I had to admit she was talented.

Damn.

They had already replaced me.

***

When I got home, I did my homework, ate dinner, and watched TV. I was bored. Normally, I would go home after practice and eat my dinner while doing my homework, and then go to bed. I was never bored because there was no time for that. This was a big adjustment.

Mom was still a little stony toward me. She silently plunked down our dinner offerings... chicken nuggets, French fries and a Jello fruit salad. That just about said it all. My brother was pretty happy. He grinned all the way through dinner and stuck his tongue out at me when our parents weren't looking.

Lovely. For a ten-year-old, his maturity level was pretty much on track with his taste in food. That old adage about boys developing and maturing more slowly than girls was definitely right-on in his case.

I went up to my room early and got ready for bed.

Snuggling down into my comfy mattress, I pulled a blanket over me, and got out the book I was reading for my AP American Lit class. We were reading *The Great Gatsby* by F. Scott Fitzgerald. It was a good story, but for the life of me, I couldn't understand Gatsby's attraction to Daisy. Her character was so shallow and silly to me; maybe even a little empty. I started to think that maybe that's what being normal was all about. The more I tried to hide my true self from others, the emptier I felt inside. I snuggled further down into my blankets, and adjusted my book in front of me. It wasn't long before I fell asleep.

The lid creaked open. The pale, sweaty man hovered over me.

"You don't look as pretty anymore," he whined disappointedly in his high, reedy voice. "I'm not having as much fun with you now that you're not as pretty."

I was scared—no… terrified.

My breathing was quick and labored. I wasn't getting much oxygen in the box. And now I was realizing that maybe he meant to kill me after all.

"Well, it's decided then…"

I woke up, breathing hard.

The light in my room was on. I looked at my alarm clock. 3:00 a.m. I got up and went to the bathroom, came back and crawled into my bed. I began to realize that this was a premonition and would probably happen to me … but when? In my vision, I knew that I was walking when I was abducted—and I was alone. Fear flooded my system; a coldness that spread from my head to my toes. I made a resolution not to walk anywhere by myself; not until this premonition or whatever it was went away. It took me a full hour to get back to sleep. When I awoke the next morning, my bedside lamp was still on.

***

I rode the bus to school, declining the offer from my mom to drive me. I didn't want another tongue-lashing in the car. I was pretty sure I would have heard the same lecture about being careful and staying out of harm's way.

After that, the first part of the day at school was uneventful. Except for the teacher telling us that Justin was still out with pneumonia. Apparently, it was a really bad case that had him in the hospital for a couple of weeks now. I had almost forgotten about him. The image I had of his lungs filling up with fluid was correct. I felt both smug and a little bothered by the fact that I had been right. I was really glad that I had convinced him to see a doctor, but I was kind of upset by the fact that there was something to the flood of information I had been getting. It scared me. I felt an overwhelming sense of responsibility. Would I have to try and save *everyone* I was getting information about? If that were the case, I would never be able to get anything done for myself. I'd be exhausted trying to fix everyone else's problems.

In the hallway between classes, Aya and I walked past the Newport High trophy case. The case was huge, but for some reason, I'd never really taken much notice of it before. There were four glass shelves, maybe eight or nine feet wide, loaded with trophies of all shapes and sizes. This time, I noticed something out of the corner of my eye.

Shiny, brighter than the rest—it practically sparkled.

It was a large football "Outstanding Player" trophy from 1979. Inscribed on the gold plate on the front of it was the name of the star quarterback, John Cook. The name vibrated with energy. John Cook... where had I heard that name before?

John Cook. The boyfriend of the girl in the hallway. 1979. I gasped.

Aya looked at me. "What's wrong?"

I stared at the trophy.

"John Cook."

"What?" Aya asked, confused.

"The name on the trophy," I repeated. "John Cook. I swear I talked to a girl in the hallway the other day who said she was looking for her boyfriend, John Cook."

She squinted at the glass. "It says 1979, Jenny. She must have been talking about someone at a different school."

"No—she said he went to *this* school," I muttered.

Aya looked at me like I was crazy. "O...kay." She started walking again.

I looked up and noticed Madeline Coalfield staring at me. I looked away, trying to seem nonchalant. I could feel her eyes on my back as Aya and I walked to class.

Chapter 9

It was the last Monday of February—two and a half weeks since my fall from the pyramid, though it seemed longer. The days had marched on, each one like the day before, monotonously creeping toward the first indication of spring. Even with the onset of more and more visions and flashes of insight I was getting, I was bored. Bored, bored, bored. I missed cheerleading. I missed the friendship, the teamwork, the activity. I noticed my bond with Julia and Aya fading a little.

Hannah and I were still fairly close, but she hung out with Julia and Aya a lot too. They were less and less inclined to invite me out to parties or to the movies. Was our friendship only based on the common tie of cheerleading? I couldn't believe that what we meant to each other was so superficial. We'd been friends since preschool. Maybe I was letting my new "strangeness" peek through my exterior somehow. I was so careful about not letting anyone know about my affliction. I tried not to show my surprise whenever I ran into a ghost or learned about someone's entire life while bumping into them in the hallway, but somehow people *sensed* something different in me, and it repelled them. As if their own intuition warned them to stay away. How ironic.

In the afternoon, while walking to my Art and Design class, I noticed a poster on the wall.

AUDITIONS

Come audition for our June production of *Into the Woods*, a musical by Stephen Sondheim.

Where: Performing Arts Hall

When: Monday, March 2nd, 3:00 p.m. – 6:00 p.m.

Requirements: Prepare a 1 minute monologue and 16 bars of music. You must bring the sheet music with you. Please come prepared.

Sign up for an audition today!

There were already a few names on the list. I saw Madeline Coalfield's name on the 3:10 p.m. slot. On a whim, I grabbed the pen hanging from the sign-up sheet and put my name below Madeline's for 3:15.

I had no idea why I put my name down. I wasn't even sure I could sing. Could I? I sang in the shower, but I didn't think I had ever sung in front of anybody else— certainly not in front of an audience. I was already regretting having put my name down and had signed it in ink, not pencil! Damn! I couldn't even erase it! But I *could* scratch it out.

Just as I was grabbing the pen to cross out my name, Madeline stepped in beside me.

"Hey!" she said excitedly. "You're auditioning for the play! That's great!" She was genuinely happy that I was auditioning.

"Actually," I shrugged, "I was just thinking that I should cross my name off."

She grabbed my arm. "No!"

I removed her hand from my arm. "Why not?"

She looked embarrassed and wiped her palms on her jeans.

"Truthfully, I was kind of hoping we'd be friends." She looked up quickly, carefully gauging my reaction to her confession.

"That day in the park—I thought we had a connection. I thought we could be friends. I know I have a lot of theatre friends, and they're great, don't get me wrong!" The words just tumbled out of her mouth nervously. "But I miss Callie so much. When I talked to you in the park, I felt… I felt like there was a spark of friendship there." Her voice trailed off. There were tears in her eyes.

I swallowed. I felt her sorrow deep down in my chest. It was gut-wrenching, emotional pain.

"God, I'm so sorry," I said, grabbing her hand. I was quiet for a moment and then I said, "I'll do it. I'll audition."

Her face brightened. "Really?"

"Really." Oh boy, what had I gotten myself into? "Here's the problem though… I've never auditioned for anything—well, except for cheerleading try-outs. I have no idea what to do."

"I'll help you!" she said. "I can play the piano, and help find a song that's perfect for you. Oh, and I have a great book of monologues. Don't worry, we'll do this together."

She looked so happy. I couldn't let her down and cross my name off the list. What was the worst thing that could happen? I wouldn't get a part. That wouldn't be so bad. I could just forget about it and join the Debate Team. Ugh. Maybe that *would* be bad. I really needed to find out what other "safe" after-school activities there were to be had.

I met up with Hannah, Julia, and Aya at our lockers after school. They were rushing to get their stuff ready for practice. Where was I rushing off to? Home. To be bored.

"Hey there!" Julia said as she stuffed her Physics book into her backpack. "I saw you talking to that drama girl in the hall. Did you sign up to audition for the school play?"

"Oh, God," Aya groaned. "Don't do that! Theatre people are such freaks."

"Not all of them," Hannah protested. "Derek Barry is kind of cute."

"Ugh." Julia rolled her eyes. "He is NOT. He wears a scarf around his neck—all the time."

I grinned and turned to Hannah. "Maybe if I get a part, I'll hook you up with him."

Hannah shrugged and a sly smile turned up the corners of her mouth. "Okay!"

I gave Julia a smug look. "See … Hannah likes theatre kids."

"Not all of them!" protested Hannah.

Julia smirked back at me. "They're freaks," she mouthed.

I felt a surge of anger and snapped, "And how do you think they view *us*? As snotty, spoiled, shallow, cheerleaders?"

Aya's mouth fell open.

"Well," Julia barked back, "Why would *you* care how they view *us*? You're not even a cheerleader anymore—you're not one of us."

I was speechless. I stared at her incredulously.

"That was below the belt, Julia," Hannah muttered.

Aya blinked. Julia herself looked shocked that she had said such a thing.

Her hand flew up to her mouth in horror. "Sorry," she whispered.

I grabbed my backpack and walked away—leaving them to stare at me as I disappeared in the flow of students exiting the building.

***

I went home, feeling sorry for myself. Was this the end of our friendship? All those years together… forgotten? Dismissed? Of all the shallow, judgmental… no, I wasn't going to go there.

I went into the kitchen to make some hot chocolate. As I reached for the marshmallows, a knock on the door startled me.

"Who could that be?" I said out loud. Jackson was at soccer practice. Mom and Dad were still at work. Maybe it was Aya, Julia, and Hannah. Maybe they had come to apologize. I let myself get my hopes up and hurried to open the door.

Madeline Coalfield stood on the doorstep holding a stack of sheet music and a monologue book in her arms.

She must have seen the disappointed look on my face because she quickly said, "Oh—if this is a bad time, I can come back later!"

"No." I recovered quickly. "No, this is a great time actually, my family isn't home yet."

She looked relieved. "Oh, good!"

"Hey, I was just making some hot chocolate. Want some?" I asked as I led her into the kitchen.

"Sure! I love hot chocolate."

She sat down while I got out two mugs and spooned some of the mix into them. "Whatcha got there?" I glanced at the sheet music.

"I brought *Castle on a Cloud* from *Les Miserables*, *Popular* from Wicked, *Good Morning Baltimore* from *Hairspray*, and *Reflection* from *Mulan*."

I took the stack and looked at the music. I had taken piano lessons up until my freshman year, so luckily I could read music. I wondered if I could actually sing the notes instead of play them.

"Do you have a piano?"

"Yes, it's in the living room."

We finished our hot chocolate and left the kitchen.

"Let's see, which one of these would suit you best?" She flipped through the pages. "How 'bout if you sing through all of them and see which one you like best?"

I shrugged.

She sat down at the piano and started with *Castle on a Cloud*. After I sang the last note, she turned from the piano and stared at me.

"What? Was I really that bad?"

"Wow," she said.

"Wow, that was terrible? Or wow, you aren't as bad a singer as I thought you would be?"

"No," she said breathlessly. "Wow, that was amazing. Wow, wow, wow, wow!!!"

"Really?"

"Yes! Really. Have you been taking singing lessons?"

I shook my head.

"You're not even in choir. I can't believe this."

"Me neither." I had never given singing a moment's thought. I'd only focused on cheerleading.

"God! Wait until Ms. Nakamura sees you audition. She will pee her pants. It's really hard to even find kids who sing in tune, let alone someone who can belt like you can."

The compliment made my cheeks flush.

"Let's try something else." She sat back down at the piano and we went through the rest of the music.

"I think I like *Reflection* the best," I said decidedly. "I feel more of a connection with it than I did with the others."

"I agree," Madeline said. "That one suits you best and really shows off your high range."

"What about a monologue?" I asked.

"I've found what works for me is to pick a monologue that's opposite from your song. So, if you pick a sad or dramatic song, you might want to pick a funny monologue to show that you are versatile."

I chose a humorous monologue. I practiced it a couple of times with her. She gave me lots of tips on how to make use of the stage and how to act out the scene.

As she was gathering all of her sheet music together, something shiny fell on the hardwood floor and twirled around until it came to a stop. A bracelet. Madeline didn't really notice since she was busy collecting her sheet music.

I bent down and picked it up.

Flash.

A man, buying the bracelet in a little shop.

It was silver, shaped like an Indian-style bear. The head was on one side and a bear claw on the other. It looked like it could be an Alaskan or Pacific Northwest Indian design. He was smiling as he paid the clerk.

The man—her dad, gave the bracelet to a little girl with dark hair. She was ecstatic. He knelt down and hugged her.

Gray skies and beautiful mountains, the ocean, little islands, eagles flying overhead.

The girl ... growing up, now in a different place, going to middle school ... Tyee Middle School? Here in Bellevue?

I recognized her. A younger version of Callie Shoemaker.

Now she was older, going to Newport High School. She was walking to the bus stop. I slipped into her body. I was her. Suddenly, I smelled that same medicinal smell— right over my nose. I couldn't breathe. As I lost consciousness, the last thing I felt was my bracelet slipping off my arm.

"Jenny? Jenny?" I heard from far away. "Jenny?"

Madeline shook me awake. I was on the floor, flat on my back.

I opened my eyes and my body shook uncontrollably.

"Jenny! Oh my God!" Madeline's worried face hovered over me. She helped me to sit up. "What happened? Are you okay?"

I sucked air rapidly in through my nose, the bracelet still clenched in my hand.

"I'll be right back!" Madeline ran to the kitchen and came back a moment later with a glass of water.

I took it and sipped it carefully, trying to control my shallow breathing.

"The bracelet," I croaked.

She looked at me quizzically. "Yes, I dropped it. Did you get dizzy picking it up?"

I shook my head. "Does it belong to you?" I asked.

"No …" she hesitated. "It belongs to Callie. Her mom let me borrow it after, you know… after she disappeared. I just needed something of hers to hold on to."

Oh my God. Was this the thing that was always nagging at the back of my mind? My worst fears confirmed… the world came crashing down on me. The realization was immediate and undeniable.

I started to shake, breaking out into a cold sweat.

"Jenny, what's going on?" Madeline asked. "Tell me." She knelt down and cradled my cheek in her hand.

I blinked back the tears that were starting to well up in my eyes. This couldn't be happening.

I debated whether or not I should tell her anything. After all, I had kept this a secret for so long. But now it was different. Now a girl's life was at stake. If I didn't come clean to someone, Callie could die… if she wasn't dead already.

"Madeline," I whispered. "I have to tell you something."

"Go ahead, I'm listening."

"It's about me. And it's about Callie."

She raised her eyebrows. "You and Callie? I don't understand. Callie doesn't know you."

I shook my head, trying to figure out a way to tell her.

I sighed. "Okay, the bracelet…"

She nodded, encouraging me to continue.

"When you dropped it on the floor, I picked it up. Once I touched it, I saw something."

61

"You saw something? What do you mean?"

I took a deep breath and blew it out.

"I saw a man buying the bracelet for a little girl with dark hair. He bought it in a little shop somewhere on the coast. Somewhere with eagles and islands..."

Madeline stared at me.

"Then I saw the girl growing up, moving, and going to school here. It was Tyee Middle School. And I recognized the girl. It was Callie."

"What are you talking about?" she whispered.

"Madeline. I have a gift. I can see things that most people can't see."

"What?"

I could tell I wasn't being clear enough. "I'm psychic."

"What … what do you mean? What does this have to do with Callie? What do you mean, you're psychic? Is this is a joke?" she stammered.

"No. I wish it was. I never wanted this. But, it is what it is. What I'm trying to tell you is that I'm psychic. And the bracelet… touching it made me realize something about Callie."

"Wait, I'm confused," Madeline said. "I still don't…" She shook her head in bewilderment.

"Okay, let me try to explain." I started again. "I've been psychic ever since I can remember. I completely pushed it away—I ignored my ability. I didn't want it. But then, I saw something when I did the flip off the pyramid. I fell because I had a vision right when I jumped. It was so intense. I thought it was a premonition about me. I thought someone was going to come after me. And I'm seeing more things, horrible things… and now I realize what I am seeing. It's about Callie, not me." The words came tumbling out.

The shocked look on Madeline's face stopped my next words. I had a moment of déjà vu, remembering my mom with the same look on her face when she realized that I had predicted her father's death.

"Oh my God!" Madeline said breathlessly.

This was the part I had been dreading. She was going to run screaming out of the house and tell everyone at school what a complete loser freak I was.

Instead, she grabbed my arm and led me over to the couch and sat me down.

"What did you see about Callie? Tell me everything! No..." she shook her head, practically arguing with herself. "No—you need to come to my house and tell my *dad* everything."

Now it was my turn to be shocked. "Your dad? What?"

She fished in her pocket and drew out her cell phone. She speed-dialed and put the phone to her ear.

"Dad? Oh good, you're home. Stay where you are. I'm bringing someone over to talk to you about Callie— someone who might know where she is." She listened for a moment and said. "Uh huh... No, don't pick me up. We're just a few minutes away. We'll be right there."

She disconnected and stood up.

"Come on!" she barked. "Get up! Get your shoes on and grab your coat."

I stood up, dazed. She grabbed my arm and yanked me to the front door. I snapped out of it and opened the hall closet and got out my coat and put it on. She opened the door. I shoved my feet into my red Converse sneakers and we rushed out of the house.

We didn't talk on the way to her place. It seemed like seconds went by, and then we were there.

As we approached the tan two-story house, the front door opened and I saw Madeline's dad step out onto the porch. He was big—about six-foot-four and maybe two-hundred pounds. His sandy blonde hair was cut short and was graying at the temples.

Madeline grabbed my arm and pushed me forward. "Dad, this is Jenny Crumb. She goes to Newport High School and lives just down around the corner, a few blocks. Jenny, this is my dad, Detective Coalfield."

"Hi, Jenny," he stuck out his hand to shake mine. "Madeline says you have some information about Callie?"

I glanced at Madeline. She had a fierce look of determination on her face, as if she was willing me to tell her dad exactly where Callie was.

"Well, I guess I do," I said uncertainly.

"Come on, let's talk about this inside." Detective Coalfield led me to the door.

We entered the cozy living room, painted a warm butterscotch color. The leather couch and armchairs were a classic shade of mahogany.

"Have a seat," Detective Coalfield gestured toward the leather chair next to the stone fireplace.

I sat down while Madeline and her dad sat on the couch opposite me.

Settling down into the chair, I tried to figure out what to say. How would I explain this without seeming like a raging lunatic?

Detective Coalfield studied my face for a few moments before he began.

"So, Madeline said you may have some information regarding Callie's disappearance. Can you tell me where you heard this information? Did you overhear someone talking or bragging about it?"

"No." I looked down at my shoes.

I could feel Madeline's impatience bubbling up within her. "Dad, she's psychic."

Detective Coalfield's eyebrows shot up in surprise. "Psychic?"

Oh my God. He was going to kick me out of here. And then he'd probably call my parents, and they'd check me into a mental hospital and...

64

Madeline broke me out of my panic. "Jenny—tell him everything from the beginning."

I sighed and took a deep breath, trying to regain composure.

"Okay, I'm psychic. Nobody knows."

"Go on," Detective Coalfield prodded.

"So, the night of the big game—I'm a cheerleader... well, I *was* a cheerleader. I climbed on top of the pyramid and did my flip. And the second I was in the air, I had a vision. Actually, I call them flashes, because that's usually how they seem to me."

"What did you see?" he asked gently.

"I saw a pale-faced man hovering over me with a knife." I swallowed.

"And then what?"

"Well, then I hit the floor and woke up in the hospital... I'm sure you heard," I said, glancing at Madeline.

"I told him about that."

"So, how does this all relate to Callie?" he asked.

I swallowed again. "Well, since then, I've been seeing flashes of this man, and he's kidnapped someone. I didn't know who the someone was. I thought I was having a premonition or something. Like maybe he was coming to get *me*. Because when I see him, I'm seeing him through the eyes of someone. But when Madeline dropped Callie's bracelet on the floor at my house and I picked it up... something made me realize that it was Callie who was with the man and not me."

He looked surprised again. "And the something that made you realize this was..."

I recounted what I had seen when I had picked up the bracelet. When I got to the part about how Callie was walking to the bus stop and the strange medicinal smell over her nose, and the bracelet slipping off her wrist, I saw

65

Detective Coalfield's demeanor change. He went from slightly relaxed and patient to hyper-aware and agitated.

He scooted to the edge of the couch and hissed, "Did you see the person with Callie? Do you know who he is or where they are?"

"No, I didn't see him that time. But I think I've been seeing him in flashes. What I think is that he's kidnapped her and has buried her underground."

Madeline gasped.

"Is she alive?" he asked.

"I think so—but maybe not for long." I explained how he had been bringing her a little water and food, but that he seemed unhappy with her now because she wasn't as pretty as she was before he kidnapped her.

"Oh, God," Madeline whimpered. "Dad, you have to find her!"

Her dad patted her knee reassuringly. "I'll do everything I can, honey."

He turned back to me. "Let's go over this a couple of times. I need you to try and remember every detail. Can you describe this man to me?"

"He's got greasy dark brown hair. The bangs are kind of long and stringy and sometimes they hang over his eyes a little. He's got pale skin, kind of ashy—like he spends lots of time indoors."

"How old do you think he is?" the detective asked.

"Ummm… I'd say he's maybe in his forties or early fifties. It's difficult for me to tell."

"How about his build? How much do you think he weighs and how tall?"

"That's hard. When I see him he's usually crouching down over me, so I don't know how tall he is. But he's got kind of a medium build, like he's maybe thin and wiry. Strong, but not muscle-bound. Oh—his eyes. They're kind of different."

"Different?"

66

"Yeah, they're brown, but not the chocolate brown that most brown-eyed people have. They're a light brown; a honey-brown. And they're really creepy... almost like they could look into you." I shuddered.

"Do you think that if I took you down to the station, you could look at some pictures and see if you can identify him?"

"I could try, but I've got to talk to my parents first. I have to tell them where I'm going." Or tell them *something*. I had no idea if I should tell them this news or if I should keep it to myself for now.

"Call them," Madeline said.

Detective Coalfield stood up. "Come on, Madeline, let's give Jenny some privacy."

They walked out of the living room and went into the kitchen.

I pulled my phone out and sat with it on my lap.

Now what? What would they do if I told them? The thought of my mother coming unglued was unsettling. They just went through the trauma of my accident. Did they really need this? Did they really need to find out that I'm psychic—and that I knew something about the missing girl everyone had been talking about? No.

I dialed my mom's cell number.

"Mom?"

"Hi, Jenny. Hey, where are you?"

"I'm calling from Madeline Coalfield's house. She just lives around the corner from us. Is it all right if I stay over here for a couple of hours? I finished my homework in study hall today."

"Oh, okay. Will you be home by 8:00 for dinner?"

"Sure, I'll be home by then," I said. It was 6:00 now. I sure hoped that two hours at the station was enough.

"Okay then," my mom said. "Have a good time. See you at 8:00."

"Love you, Mom."

67

"Love you too, Jenny."

I disconnected and walked over to the kitchen.

"All cleared to go to the station?" Detective Coalfield asked.

"Yup. Let's go," I said.

Madeline and I got into the back of her dad's unmarked, charcoal gray sedan. We drove in silence to the police station. The sky had darkened and I shivered, wishing that I had brought a heavier jacket.

When we arrived, I sat down in a conference room with a long table and eight chairs. Madeline sat down to my right. Detective Coalfield brought in two big binders, filled with the booking pictures of criminals.

I opened the book and started flipping through the pages.

The faces looking up at me through those pages terrified me. One after the other... I saw horrifying image after image. Stabbing, strangling, shooting... I saw each crime they had committed, each victim screaming in pain and terror. I slammed the books closed. Sweat was pouring down my face and I was breathing rapidly.

Detective Coalfield, who was standing behind his daughter, leaned over and grabbed my arm. "Jenny, are you okay?"

I shook my head. "No, I'm not."

"Did you recognize the man who took Callie?" Madeline asked hopefully.

"No, I'm sorry. It's just that every face I see... I see the crimes these guys committed. The images are so awful!" Tears welled up in my eyes.

"You see the crimes associated with the photos?" Detective Coalfield asked.

I wiped the tears away with my sleeve.

"Wow—that's a really powerful ability you've got there," he said. "Wish I had your gift. My job would be so much easier."

"It wasn't always like this," I admitted. "It's been getting more and more intense over the past couple of years."

"Are you able to turn off the scary images when you want to?" Madeline asked.

I was shocked by her question. I'd never even given that a thought.

"No," I answered. "I mean, in the past, I was able to push it away and ignore it, but I've never been able to shut it off completely."

"Try it," she urged. She opened one of the books and scooted it closer to me. Immediately, the images flooded my head. I panicked—the feelings and images were overwhelming. I tried to shut them down... tried to push them away. I couldn't do it.

Crying, I closed the book with a bang.

"I can't!" I shoved the book away from me.

"Oh my God. I'm sorry," Madeline put her arm around me. "I didn't mean to push. I just wanted to find the guy who took Callie. I want her back!" She burst into tears.

Detective Coalfield, looking helpless, patted both of us on the shoulders.

"It's okay, Jenny," he said. "I think I might be able to help you."

I looked up at him. "What do you mean?"

"Well, sometimes when I can't get any leads on a case, I ask for help. There's a woman in Seattle who helps me out on those cases. She's a psychic."

"You work with a psychic?" I asked, not believing what I was hearing.

"Yes, I do. Don't look so shocked!" he said, smiling. "Why do you think I didn't laugh at you when you told me about your ability? I would imagine that most people wouldn't believe you if you told them."

"Or," I said ruefully, "They would think that I am a freak or a weirdo."

"Maybe."

"Well, I don't think that," Madeline insisted. "I think that everybody has a little psychic ability. And some people just have a whole lot more than others."

"Really?" I asked. "You don't think I'm a freak?"

"No!" She wiped the tears from her cheeks. "No, I don't think that at all."

Detective Coalfield walked across the room and pulled the tissue box off the window ledge. He came back and put the box between Madeline and me.

A thought occurred to me just then. "Wait—if you work with a psychic on difficult cases, why haven't you contacted *her* about Callie's case?"

"I have," he answered. "But she couldn't get anything. She tried holding on to one of Callie's shirts, she looked at her picture, and... nothing. That doesn't happen very often."

"Weird," I said. "So, how do you think she can help me?"

"You're going to think this sounds silly," he said, "but she actually has a school for people who want to perfect their psychic ability."

"You have got to be kidding me!" I said, shocked at the existence of some kind of psychic academy.

"Nope, not kidding."

"So, how could she help me? I've got plenty of psychic ability. In fact, I've got too much. It drives me crazy!"

"That's what I mean," he explained. "She may be able to help you control your gift, so it doesn't drive you crazy."

I thought about that for a minute. "Well, if she can do that, she would be a saint."

He pulled his cell phone out of his pocket and dialed.

70

"Celine? Hi, it's Detective Coalfield. Hey, I have someone here who needs your help. Can you make time to meet with her? It's related to the Callie Shoemaker case— it's urgent." He listened. "Okay, let me ask."

He covered the mouthpiece with his hand. "Jenny, she's canceling her appointments tomorrow and can meet with you right after school. Are you okay with that?"

"Why can't she meet right now? Isn't it an emergency?"

"Actually, she's dealing with another emergency right now—she's working with a detective from another police department on a homicide case."

That made me wonder if there were lots of psychics out there working with the police. If the media found out about this, there would be a full-fledged frenzy on every station.

I shrugged. "Sure, I don't have anything after school."

"Yes, she can meet at—let's say, 3:30 or 4:00. I'll drive her over there myself. See you then." He put his phone back in his pocket.

"It's a go. Let's get you two back home so you can do your homework and have dinner. Jenny, I'll drop you off at your house."

"Thanks," I said, wondering what would happen tomorrow.

Chapter 10

After school the next day, I caught the bus home and tried to do some homework. In truth, I didn't get much done. I was too nervous about my meeting with Celine the psychic. And I could scarcely think of anything else but Callie—whether or not she was alive, and how I would be able to help her. I called both my mom and dad at work and told them that I would be studying with friends until dinner.

At around 3:00 p.m., Detective Coalfield and Madeline showed up at the door. I grabbed a notebook and pencil, my jacket, and my cell phone and locked the door behind me.

We drove to downtown Seattle and miraculously found a parking spot on 3rd and Pike. We only had to walk a block down to Celine's apartment building.

My heart was racing when we buzzed her apartment. There was an electronic beep and then the light by the door flashed green. Detective Coalfield opened the heavy door and we stepped into the inner courtyard. He led us up one flight of stairs and down the hallway to apartment 202.

Sensing my nervousness, Madeline grabbed my arm, trying to reassure me.

As we approached her place, the door opened and Celine stepped out, waving to us. She was not what I expected. For some reason, I had pictured her to be an older lady, overweight, wearing a flowing New-Agey outfit with lots of jewelry dangling everywhere. She was the polar opposite of what I had imagined.

Standing about five feet, seven inches tall, she was just a bit taller than me. She was thin, had shoulder length light brown hair, and startlingly light blue eyes. She had such a warm smile that I found myself smiling back. I reached out my hand to shake hers, but she rushed forward and hugged me instead.

"Welcome, welcome!" she beamed. She stepped back from me and hugged Detective Coalfield and Madeline. "Come in."

We walked into the living room where an antique sofa and two arm chairs were cozily arranged around a mahogany coffee table. The smell of incense permeated the room.

"I'm so glad I could meet you today! My clients were disappointed for the short-notice cancellations, but this is important. It can't wait," she said as her smile faded a bit.

She whisked into her kitchen, which was open to the living room. She placed a teapot, four delicate tea cups, and four spoons on an antique silver tray, along with a dainty pitcher of cream and a dish with sugar cubes piled high. She brought the tray over and set it on the coffee table.

"Tea?" she asked, pouring the first cup of steaming amber liquid. "Help yourself to the cream and sugar."

We each took a cup as she filled them and stirred in our cream and sugar. I wondered if tea was Detective Coalfield's drink of choice or if he was just drinking it out of politeness.

After Celine and had fixed her own cup of tea, she looked directly at me, her light blue eyes drilling a hole through me.

"Now, what can I help you with?" she asked.

Everyone in the room looked at me. "Uh …"

"Jenny has a gift," Detective Coalfield interrupted.

"Mmmmhmmmm..." she said, sipping her tea.

"Well, it's a very powerful gift, in my humble opinion. She has some information about the Shoemaker case, but her gift is kind of getting in the way."

"In the way?" Celine raised her eyebrows.

"There's too much extraneous information coming in from other sources, and she can't filter out what she needs."

He went on to explain everything that had happened so far, including the incident at the police station where I couldn't look through the books without having all of the images overwhelm me.

"Yes, that's quite common in someone who has an ability this powerful. It happened to me when I was her age."

"It did?" I asked in surprise.

"Yes, it did. It was really terrifying. But luckily, I had my mom to help me. She's psychic too."

"Oh! I didn't know that it was a genetic thing. Wait, *is* it a genetic thing?" I asked.

"Well, it certainly *can* be. Many of my students have parents who are psychic—and some of them either don't realize it or they don't want to admit it," she said, directing her gaze at me.

I coughed and reached for my tea. "Well, I don't think my parents are psychic."

"Would you know if they were?" she asked.

"I guess I wouldn't really know... if they chose to hide it from me." I mulled over the possibility. I thought of all the times I had hidden my gift from my family and friends.

Detective Coalfield interrupted us. "Is there a way to help Jenny focus only on the information she needs to help find Callie?"

"Yes, there are ways, techniques that can help. Detective, why don't you take Madeline down to Pike

74

Place Market for a bit and do some shopping? I'd like to work with Jenny alone for an hour or so. Is that all right with you?"

He stood. "Sure."

Madeline got up nervously. "Are you sure it's okay?" she whispered to me.

"Yes, I'll be fine," I said. Surprisingly, I meant it. I wasn't afraid of this woman. How could I be? She was completely normal and… nice.

Madeline and her dad went out the door. Celine closed it and sat back down in her arm chair. She crossed her legs and tugged her cardigan down.

"So, now I understand why I was drawing a blank on the Callie Shoemaker case." She gave me an appraising look.

"Huh?" I asked, taking the bait.

"Because I was supposed to meet you—to help you. You're the one getting the information. I need to help you sort it all out, and get you on the right track with your gift."

For some reason, that caught me by surprise. This was supposed to happen? If I was predestined to meet Celine, was the rest of my life already planned out too?

I didn't like thinking about that. It seemed too fatalistic—like I had no control over how my life would turn out. But, maybe this part of my life *was* planned, and that was a good thing. Because anything that could help save Callie's life was good, even if it meant exposing my secret.

Celine interrupted my thoughts. "I want to show you a technique for sorting out the information you *do* want from the information you *don't* want."

"Oh yeah, that would be really great! I mean, if I didn't have to see all that scary stuff, I would be really, really, happy."

"Well, I can't promise you that you won't see *all* those scary images. You will see some; you can't really block it all out. But you *can* minimize or lessen the images, and that helps you to see the ones that you do want."

"Okay. Where do we start?" I asked, eager to begin.

"Before I do anything, like a reading for someone, a house blessing, or helping the police with a case, I start with a prayer," she said.

"A prayer?"

"Always. There are lots of different kinds of prayers for different circumstances, but you don't need to learn all of those at once. You'd never remember any of them. So for now, how 'bout I teach you just one or two?"

"I didn't realize it was a religious process," I said with hesitation. I felt a little awkward. Although everyone in my family believed in God, we never attended church or really even talked about spirituality. It was an unknown area to me.

"It's not a religious process, but it's definitely a spiritual process. We are all connected to God or our higher power. The more in tune we can be with Spirit, the more fulfilling our lives can be. To be present with ourselves means we can be connected more easily with God. I know it's a foreign concept for you. I can tell you're uncomfortable—but trust me; you don't have to believe it at first. I think you will come to believe it the more you can access that connection to God."

I shrugged. "Okay, I guess."

Her musical laughter burst out of her in delight. "It's going to be okay, I promise!"

"All right, I'll give it a try."

"First though, I want to start with a prayer to ask Spirit, that's what I call God, to help me to help you. I'll ask Spirit to help us both on our journey. You don't have to remember this prayer. It's actually more of a song, a hymn. So close your eyes and just listen."

She was going to sing? Awkward. She closed her eyes, but I kept mine open for a moment as she began to hum. It did sound like a hymn—very melodic and simple. It was quite beautiful actually. After a minute or so, I closed my eyes, feeling a little more comfortable. The hymn was soothing; I didn't know why I had been so worried about it.

As I relaxed, the hymn became more of a chant and she added words. It sounded like a very long string of words in foreign languages and after listening for a bit, I realized that I recognized some of those words... they were the names for "God" in other religions. She then asked for Spirit's blessing for us.

"Spirit, I ask that you help me to guide Jenny in her journey. Help her to use her gift for the greater good. Help her to find Callie."

We both opened our eyes. "Now then, Jenny," she said, reaching under her chair where a copy of the Seattle Times lay. "Let's do an exercise."

She laid the newspaper on my lap. "What do you see?"

I looked down at the front page. There was a picture of young man with a ring through his eyebrow. Next to his picture, there was a picture of a teenage girl. The headline read, "SUSPECT ARRESTED IN STABBING DEATH OF MELISSA JONES."

Flash.

There was a man and a girl in a car with two other young men. Rap music was blaring loudly in the background, the bass turned up to the max, shaking the car as they drove. The girl and the guy in the backseat were arguing, his breath smelled of beer. The guy pulled a screwdriver out from behind the car cushions. Without warning, he whipped the screwdriver in front of him and stabbed the girl in the neck. Blood sprayed everywhere, splattering on the seats and windows.

I yelped.

"Jenny?" Celine interrupted, taking the paper back.

I shook my head violently. "Oh my God."

"Take a deep breath," Celine instructed.

I took a breath and closed my eyes, trying to clear the image.

"Now, I want you to imagine a white light surrounding you, protecting you. Imagine that it covers you and radiates out at least two feet from your body. Now imagine a golden cord that reaches down from heaven, from God, reaching down to you, connecting you to love and safety. Each time you do this, you only have to remember to visualize the white light around you. The cord, in this instance, is your initial tie into Spirit."

I imagined the white light around me. Then, the cord spiraling out of heaven and connecting me to safety and love. My breathing slowed and deepened.

"Better?" she asked.

I nodded.

"Good. Now repeat after me. Let the white light of the Holy Spirit surround and protect me."

I repeated, "Let the white light of the Holy Spirit surround and protect me."

She continued. "Spirit, I ask that you only show me the things that I *need* to know."

After I repeated the last line, she handed the paper back to me. "Now, try it again."

I looked at the paper. There was a cloudy image of what had happened to the girl, Melissa—so I knew what had happened to her. But the image wasn't nearly as strong as before. I didn't see the actual stabbing and I didn't see the spray of blood. I just got the impression or a summary of what had happened.

I grinned in relief. "It worked!"

"You are a quick study," she said. "Usually, it takes many more times to teach this technique. You're quite amazing!"

"Thanks," I said.

"So, now that you've got the hang of it, anytime you are bombarded with images like that, I want you to repeat that process. Take a deep breath, close your eyes and ask for help. By the way, you don't have to say it out loud if there are other people around. Saying it silently in your head will suffice."

"Oh good." I sighed. "People would think I'm nuts going around and saying stuff like that all day."

"Sometimes you have to let go of what other people think," she said gently. "It's okay to be different."

"Yeah, but it's not okay to be a freak in high school … you have no idea!"

"I was young once too, you know. I know how kids are. But just because you're psychic doesn't mean that you are a freak." She picked up her cup, and took a sip.

I thought about that for a moment. If I told my friends that I was psychic, would they think I was a freak? Would they break their ties with me and expose me to the rest of the student population? It seemed like they already had broken ties, maybe sensing the change in me. How different I had become on the inside—even I didn't recognize me anymore. Did cheerleading define me? No, I didn't think that it did.

I would've liked to think that they would accept me and keep my secret. There really was no way of knowing what they would do. If they knew. Then a question occurred to me.

"Celine, why is it that I can't predict what my friends would do if they knew about my gift? And why is it that I can't see very much about my own *stuff*?"

"Well, it's the same for me. And I believe it's the same for all psychics. We don't get to see that much about our own lives. Certainly, we can see if we are in danger and we can have gut feelings about things. But we can't see a lot of the other stuff. For example, there are lots of psychics who choose relationships that aren't right for them. Maybe they fall for men or women who don't treat them well or take advantage of them. That's the kind of thing we have trouble with." She tucked her hair behind her ear. "It's really too bad, isn't it?"

"That really sucks," I said. "It would be nice if we could know about the relationship stuff. Wouldn't it be great if all the guys who asked you out had been prescreened by the universe or something? Then you'd be sure not to get the wrong one sent your way!"

"That would come in handy."

"Were you going to teach me another prayer?" I asked.

"Well, yes. I want you to take some quiet time each day to sit and connect with God or Spirit—use your third eye. I've found what works for me is to set aside some time each day and sit cross-legged on the floor with a white candle. Light the candle, place your hands on your knees in a meditative position, like when you do yoga. Relax your eyes and watch the flame. Try not to hold any thoughts in your head."

"Wait a minute, back up." I stopped her. "I'm confused. What is a third eye?"

"Everyone has a third eye. It's the area right between your eyes, a little above your eyebrows. And when you are able to open your third eye, your vision or insight opens up. The questions that have been lingering in your mind may be answered if Spirit wills it."

. "Does this happen every time you do this exercise?" I asked.

"No, not every time. Especially at first. You may do this ten to twenty times before you feel the connection. You just have to keep at it."

"So do I say a prayer with this?"

"If you want to, you can repeat a mantra over and over. For some people, this helps them to slide into the third eye frequency. It goes like this: Let the light that gives light to the universe enter all my being."

I got out my notebook and pencil and quickly scribbled the mantra down. I tapped the pencil point down on the paper, trying to remember the first prayer.

Without missing a beat, Celine said, "The other prayer is—let the white light of the Holy Spirit surround and protect me."

"Thanks." I scribbled that down as well. "Can I also use those mantras so I don't have to hear people's thoughts?"

"Yes, and feel free to change your prayers to suit the situation. This doesn't have to be exact. The universe will hear you, and will work on your behalf."

The door buzzed and I jumped at the noise.

"I guess our time is up," Celine announced, walking to the door to buzz them in. "Time flies when you're having fun. *Did* you have fun? Did you learn anything valuable that might help you?"

"Yeah! I learned so much from you. I feel like I could just sit here all day and learn even more. Just learning these two techniques... I think that maybe I have a chance of finding Callie." I felt like I was walking on air. Now I had some tools to use.

"Good. You can come back if you need more help. If you like, you can sign up for a class. I teach this kind of material in groups, and we actually go out into the field and test what we learned in class. It's quite useful, if I do say so myself."

I shrugged. "Yeah, I might just sign up for that. But are you also available to do more of this one-on-one kind of training? Or maybe even over the phone?"

"Sure," she said, "whatever you are comfortable with."

She went to open the door for Detective Coalfield and Madeline. They were carrying shopping bags with fresh vegetables and some seafood from the market.

"Well? Any progress?" Detective Coalfield asked.

"Yes, I want to try looking through those books again. I'm anxious to see if I can do it this time," I said.

He seemed relieved. "Well, that is really great news! How 'bout if we tackle that tomorrow? I just got a call from the station; I'm needed there right away. I have to drop Madeline off at home so she can help her mom make dinner, and I'm sure your parents are expecting you as well."

I felt weird about not jumping in and trying to find Callie right away. What if the Creepy Guy killed her?

Celine caught my eye. "It's okay. In this line of work, there is a right time for everything. When you go home, take some quiet time for yourself. You may just see something then."

We thanked Celine, and walked back to the car.

It had started drizzling, and the wipers swished the tiny drops off the windshield. I looked out the window at the gray skyline. Traffic sucked, as expected on a weekday during rush hour. Detective Coalfield got in the left-most lane getting on to I-90. From here, we could get in the carpool lanes across the floating bridge over Lake Washington, saving lots of time getting back to the eastside.

I was home by 7:00 p.m.

"Ah! There she is!" My mother beamed at me. "Just in time for dinner!"

"What are we having?"

"Mexican rice bowls—I got the salsa you like."

My brother, who came in to sit down at the kitchen table to do his homework, actually grinned. "Yes!" he said, pumping his fist up and down. "I love Mexican rice bowls!"

I laughed, feeling better than I had in weeks. It was the one thing he and I agreed on. Mexican rice bowls rocked.

As we were passing the bowl of shredded cheese around the table, Mom asked, "How was your day at school?"

"Fine," I answered simply. "Oh—I forgot to tell you. Yesterday, I signed up to audition for the school play."

"Really?" Dad asked. "I didn't know you were interested in theatre."

"I guess I didn't really give it much thought before," I replied. "I mean, I was so wrapped up in cheerleading that I didn't have time to think of anything else. But I've always gone to all of the school productions and enjoyed them, so I thought, why not?"

"What's the name of the play?" he asked.

"It's called *Into the Woods*," I said.

"*Into the Woods*?" my mom asked. "Stephen Sondheim, right? My friend Deb from work saw that a couple of years ago at 5th Avenue Theatre. She said it was fantastic!"

"Yeah, and it's a musical."

"A musical?" My brother sneered at me. "You can't sing. Why are you trying out? You'll just embarrass yourself."

I shrugged. "A friend told me that I can sing—Madeline Coalfield. She's helping me with my audition material."

"Well, I hope she's a miracle worker." He snickered and took a bite of his food.

"Cut it out, Jackson," my dad warned. "If Jenny wants to try out for the school production, we should be nothing but supportive. Just like we're supportive of you and go to all your soccer games. We cheer you on—now let's cheer Jenny on."

Jackson rolled his eyes.

"When are the auditions?" Mom asked.

"They're on Monday from 3:00 to 6:00 p.m. But mine is scheduled for 3:15. I think I'll be completely done by 3:30, but I honestly don't know how it works."

"I can come pick you up at 3:30 if you want," my dad offered. "Unless you feel up to driving again…"

"You know, I *do* feel like driving again. How 'bout if I try it this weekend and see how it goes?" I dipped a tortilla chip into my rice bowl and scooped up a bite full.

"That's the spirit!" My dad grinned and high-fived me across the table.

Chapter 11

"Come on," he said, taking my hand and pulling me up. "I need to get you cleaned up before I send the ransom note."

He pulled me up and out of the ground. It was raining. The earth was damp and smelled like rotting leaves, mushrooms, and moss. My legs were nearly useless, not having used them in God knows how long. My feet felt like weighted bags of sand.

"Walk!" he said, frustrated with my lack of progress.

"I... can't!" I moaned.

He turned toward me, his face a mask of anger, and slapped me across the face.

I screamed, sitting up in bed. I could still feel the sting across my cheek.

Footsteps sounded in the hall and the door swung open.

"Jenny! What's wrong?!" my mom said breathlessly.

I panted, sweat prickling up on my forehead. "Bad dream," I breathed out.

"Oh, honey, you are having so many bad dreams! I wonder if we should go see a doctor about this," my mom said.

"No," I said, my pulse coming back down to a more normal rate. "I'm fine. I don't even remember what the dream was about." Lying was not my strong suit, but Mom seemed to buy it.

"Well, if you're sure... are you going to be okay? Do you want me to stay here for a while?"

"No, really. I'll be fine," I answered confidently.

"Okay, if you're sure." She got up off the bed and smoothed the hair away from my forehead, kissing me lightly. She shuffled toward the door and looked back over her shoulder as she blew me another kiss. She closed the door quietly.

I looked at the clock. It was 5:30 a.m. I had to get up in an hour anyway. There was no way I could go back to sleep. I'd call Detective Coalfield at 6:30 and hope that he was awake by then. In the meantime, I turned on the light on my night stand and snuck out my bedroom door. I tiptoed down the stairs and into the living room and picked up the white candle on the fireplace mantel. I found the matches in the junk drawer in the kitchen and snuck back up to my room.

Sitting cross-legged on my cream carpeted floor, I lit the candle and put my hands in the yoga positions on my knees. I stared at the flame for a few minutes and tried to clear my mind. After a while, I felt at peace and decided to repeat the mantra I had learned the day before.

"Let the light that gives light to the universe enter all my being," I chanted quietly over and over again. I didn't know how much time had gone by, because I felt so light, so good. When I finally opened my eyes and looked at the clock, I felt refreshed and rejuvenated. It was only 6:00 a.m., so I turned on my laptop and opened up some writing homework. I had already finished it, but I wanted to give it some extra polish.

My alarm went off just as I finished rewriting the last sentence. I printed out the report and slipped it into my backpack. I found my cell phone in the top pocket of my pack and dialed Madeline's number.

"Hello?" a sleepy voice answered.

"Madeline?" I asked.

"Mmmhmm," she said.

"It's Jenny. Is your dad still at home?"

"Hold on a minute, I'll go check," she said as she went off to look. "Dad? Wait! Just a second, Jenny, he was just leaving but he's coming back to the house. Hold on."

"Hello?" Detective Coalfield answered.

"Hi, it's Jenny. Sorry to bother you, but I had another dream about Callie."

"Oh? And?" he asked directly.

"I think he's taking her somewhere to get cleaned up. He is going to send a ransom note," I said.

"A ransom note? That's odd. Usually if someone sends a ransom note, it's just a day or so after the kidnapping. Why so late? Did you pick up on anything about why it's so late?" he asked.

"No, that's it," I said.

"I'll alert Callie's parents. I'll tell them to look for a note or communication from this guy. Are you all right?" he asked, sounding concerned.

"Yes, I'm fine. I'll let you know if I get anything else."

***

School was boring, but at least I managed a little chit chat with Aya and Hannah. I even ran into Julia in the bathroom, and we were friendly with one another on a superficial level. She looked uncomfortable—like she wanted to say something, but didn't know how. I didn't have the energy to force a conversation, so I let it go.

After school, Madeline came over and we worked on our songs and monologues until Detective Coalfield knocked on the door at 4:30.

"Do you think we could run over to the station and look at those books again?" he asked. "The Shoemakers received a ransom note today—it's for three million dollars."

"Three million?" I swallowed hard. How could anyone afford that?

Madeline furrowed her brows and stamped her foot. "That's ridiculous! The Shoemakers don't have that kind of money!"

"I know. But maybe we can figure out who this guy is with a little help from Jenny. If she can identify him, it will give us a place to start looking."

I hoped and prayed with all of my might that I could identify this creep.

***

Twenty minutes later, we were sitting in the conference room again, the stack of books in front of me. I took one and pushed the others aside.

"Okay, don't think I'm weird, but Celine taught me this technique to keep the scary images from overwhelming me."

"Go ahead. We won't laugh," Madeline said with a smile. Detective Coalfield nodded with encouragement.

I closed my eyes and began. "Let the white light of the Holy Spirit surround and protect me. God, I ask that you only show me the things that I need to see to help Callie."

With my eyes still closed, I imagined myself surrounded by a beautiful radiant white glow. I felt the warmth from the light, making me feel safe and at peace.

I looked down at the stack of books, took the one off the top, and pushed the other two aside. I opened the book to the first page. An African American man in his early twenties. Nope, definitely not the creepy, sweaty guy. Next, a balding middle-aged Caucasian guy. Nope. Next, a Hispanic man in his fifties—nope.

I must have sat there for over an hour, flipping through the pages. Nope, nope, nope, nope. Nothing, nada. Crap. A single tear rolled down my right cheek.

"Are you okay?" Detective Coalfield asked. "Is it too overwhelming still?"

"No, it's not that," I answered quietly. "It's just—I was hoping I'd be able to find this guy. And he's not in here! Now what do we do?"

Madeline looked just as disappointed as I felt.

Detective Coalfield patted me on my shoulder. "It's okay, Jenny. Maybe he'll make a mistake. Maybe you'll have another dream. I know it's hard and you really want to find him. So do we. But we are all doing the best that we know how to do. I have faith that something will come up."

"You do?" I sniffed. Even though I was afraid of the visions, I now wanted nothing more than to have more of them. The more information I could pick up, the more likely it was that we could find Callie and apprehend the man who took her.

"Yes," he said encouragingly. "I believe we'll find her."

I hoped with all my heart that he was right.

***

I got home right before dinner and walked into the family room. Jackson and Dad were watching some dumb game show and were shouting out the answers.

"Hi, Jen!" Dad said. "Where have you been?"

I wasn't sure what to say so I stalled by yawning and stretching nonchalantly. "Oh, I was with Madeline Coalfield. Her dad drove me home 'cause it was dark."

"You seem to have struck up quite the friendship with her," my dad remarked.

"Yeah, she's really nice. She's auditioning for the musical as well."

"Hey! Well, that's great!" he said. "Care to sing your audition song for us?"

"Yeah, sing for us!" my brother grinned.

"No way," I said, feeling terrified at the thought.

"Why not, are you afraid?" Jackson taunted. "If you're afraid to sing in front of us, what are you going to do when you have to sing at the audition? Lip synch?"

"No, funny man, I'm not afraid. I just don't want to right now." I crossed my arms and glared at him.

Dad shrugged. "Well, I think you'll do just fine at the auditions. We support you one hundred percent."

"Thanks, Dad," I said. I plopped down on the couch next to him.

The game show ended and the news came on.

The King 5 news anchor shuffled his notes and looked up at the camera. "Good evening and thanks for joining us. Our top story tonight is the disappearance of sixteen-year-old Callie Shoemaker, who was last seen on February 6th. Authorities have received an anonymous tip indicating that the missing Newport High School student may have been kidnapped."

A school picture of Callie flashed across the screen.

I swallowed hard. Would Detective Coalfield have given the media my name?

Chapter 12

"Get in the shower!" the creepy man shouted. "God! You are so ugly now. What did I ever see in you?" He spat on the yellowed vinyl bathroom floor in disgust.

He was angry. Not just a little angry... a lot angry. I stepped into the shower stall, naked and self-consciously quivering. He was glaring at me through the textured glass shower door. A wave of humiliation and repulsion ran down my spine.

I forgot about my fear the moment I stepped into the warm stream of water. I put my head back and let the water wash away the dirt. On the floor of the shower was a bottle of shampoo and a bottle of conditioner. I picked up the bottle and popped the spout open. It was cheap shampoo, but I didn't care. It lathered up quickly in my palms and smelled like a meadow of flowers. I almost laughed. The simple act of washing my hair was so normal and yet the circumstances were so not normal. The soap was great too. The rose-colored bar was fragrant and smooth as silk. I scrubbed every last inch of me, not caring what the creep outside thought. I would stay in here forever if I could. Away from his prying eyes, his sweaty hands.

"All right! Get out!" he banged on the shower door. "You've been in there long enough." He threw a towel over the edge of the shower. He wrenched the shower door open, shut off the water, and yanked me out by the hair.

I woke up with a start. My alarm clock said it was 3:00 a.m. I grabbed my cell phone off the dresser next to my bed and dialed Detective Coalfield's number. It rang at least five times before his sleepy voice answered.

"This is Jenny. I'm really sorry to call you in the middle of the night like this, but I had another dream."

His voice sharpened and he became more alert. "What is it? What did you see?"

"He got her out of her underground cell. He took her somewhere—I think to where he lives. He's making her take a shower, getting her cleaned up. He's angry with her and is really rough with her... hurting her. He's getting her ready for something. I don't know what, though."

He cursed and muttered something indistinguishable, and then he was quiet for a moment, gathering his thoughts.

"Jenny, I want you to try and figure out if this guy knew Callie from somewhere. I'm not so sure this is just a random kidnapping. I have a hunch he may have been watching her before he took her. Is it possible to concentrate on that?" he asked.

"I don't know. I can try," I said, doubting my ability to do anything remotely useful like that.

"Work on it if you can. I'm going to try and get some sleep and then I'll go talk to Callie's parents. They are working hard to come up with the ransom money."

"I'll do my best." I wished I had more information for him. Why couldn't I come up with a piece of information he could actually use? "I'll call you if I come up with anything."

"Oh—and Jenny, I want you to concentrate on any descriptive details that you can: the house she was in, the bathroom, where the house is, and street names. Any kind of detail you remember will be useful. Write it all down and we'll talk tomorrow."

I put my cell phone on the dresser beside my bed and snuggled back down under the covers. Detective Coalfield had a hunch that this creep had been watching Callie. If that was true, where did he see her? How did he spy on her without getting caught? I had so many questions.

Instead of going back to sleep right away, I slipped out of bed and found a notebook and a pencil. I wrote down everything I could remember about the dream, including the color of the tile in the bathroom, what kind of shampoo Callie had used, the color of the soap. It didn't seem like that would help at all, but I did it anyway. I put my notebook under my bed and got under the covers. I turned out my light and fell into an uneasy sleep.

Chapter 13

The weekend came quickly. I worked on my audition song and monologue for hours on Saturday morning while my parents and brother were out making a Costco run. For some reason, Jackson liked going to Costco. Personally, I couldn't stand the place. Jackson probably just liked going there for all the free processed food samples.

After rehearsing my song for what felt like the hundredth time, I decided that I needed to give driving a try. I was nervous. I hadn't driven in several weeks. There was only one problem... I had no idea where I wanted to go. Did I need anything? Last time I checked, the fridge was stocked full. I wasn't really in need of anything. Wait a minute. Bellevue Square Mall! I hadn't gone shopping in ages—and I needed a cute outfit for the audition.

I ran upstairs and dug through my secret stash of cash in my underwear drawer. Not even Jackson would dare look for money in there. I pulled out four twenty dollar bills and put them in my purse.

I went back to the kitchen and wrote a note to my parents, telling them where I had gone.

I went out the door and locked it behind me. My car, a blue 2006 Honda Accord, was parked on the very left side of our driveway. The third bay of the garage had been turned into Dad's man cave, so of course, my car was the one left out in the driveway in all sorts of weather. That was all right with me. I was just glad to have a car.

I got in and buckled my seatbelt. I sat for a moment, getting up my nerve, and then put the key in the ignition. The engine rumbled a bit from so many weeks sitting idle while I rode the bus or with my mom. I waited until it hummed smoothly.

As I pulled out of the driveway, I kept waiting for some sort of flash or vision to throw me off my course, but nothing happened. I breathed a sigh of relief. I was driving again!

When I got to the mall, I drove slowly alongside the parking garage and turned into the entrance near Nordstrom's. A car was just pulling out of a prime parking spot near the front. Score! I whipped into the spot, feeling exhilarated. Funny how little things seemed to be making me very happy these days.

I got out and walked across the street to the mall. Maybe I would hit J. Crew first and then Nordstrom's for shoes. I guess I should have brought more money. I had a credit card that my parents gave me for emergencies. Okay, this was an emergency! I really *needed* a cute outfit and a cute pair of shoes… after all, it was for a good cause. I had to look good for the audition. I rationalized the need to spend money, and headed inside.

The minute I stepped through the doors of the mall, I felt like my body was in hyper-awareness mode. My senses were on overload as the sights, smells, and the sounds of the people and places washed over me. The smell of the Cinnabon shop nearby practically knocked me off my feet. It was almost tempting enough for me to veer off course and blow my focus on my mission. No, I was here to get an outfit. Nothing would stop me from getting my outfit, not even a delicious cinnamon roll slathered with creamy frosting.

I stuck to my guns and went up the staircase to the upper level of the mall. I noticed as I walked past the shops, different items in the windows caught my attention.

A light blue baseball cap in the window of a baseball hat shop. It was weird that I had never noticed a shop in the mall that was solely devoted to selling baseball caps. But, there it was.

Next I noticed puffy jackets, then sunglasses. They almost jumped out of the display windows at me, catching me by surprise.

"Weird," I muttered.

I finally made it to my favorite store and glided around the clothing racks, looking for just the right outfit. I had just found a really cute light green cashmere sweater when a motion out of the corner of my eye broke my concentration. I looked up and saw a man and a girl on the other side of the store. She was wearing a man's puffy ski jacket and jeans that were too big. Her long brown hair was drawn back in a ponytail and covered up with a light blue baseball cap. And the oddest thing was that she was wearing a pair of large sunglasses—in a store, in February.

My eyes shifted over to the man holding on to her elbow. He was wiry, thin, maybe about five feet ten inches. He was also wearing a baseball cap, a large parka, and sunglasses. When she moved away from him slightly, I caught a glimpse of something shiny and black in his hand. He pulled her along the racks and unexpectedly maneuvered the girl toward the corner of the store and looked up. I followed his glance upward and noticed the store security camera. He positioned her, smirked, and took off her cap and glasses for a second.

She looked absolutely terrified. Suddenly, she turned her head and looked directly at me. It was Callie.

The man's eyes followed the turn of her head. I froze. He saw the recognition in my face, the shock, and he sneered at me. He bolted, with Callie in tow.

I dropped the sweater I was holding and fished around in my coat pocket for my cell phone and tore out of the store after them.

My heart was pounding in my ears. As I ran, I flipped my phone open and speed-dialed Detective Coalfield. It rang once as I ran past the baseball cap store. Callie and the man looked back at me as they turned the corner.

My breathing was ragged and shallow, and I was near to panic. The phone rang a second time. I caught a glimpse of Callie and the man running for the staircase to the lower level of the mall. The phone rang a third time.

"This is Detective Coalfield." His voice sounded calm.

"Detective!" I panted. "I found Callie!" My breathing was irregular and I knew I must have sounded odd on the phone. I made it to the stairs and nearly hurled myself down them like a torpedo, not noticing if my feet were connecting with the steps or not.

"Jenny? What? Where are you?" he asked urgently.

"At Bellevue Square. They are running toward the big entrance doors by The North Face store."

"Bellevue Square? What? Are you sure?"

"Yes! I'm sure." Geesh. I ran out the doors. "She's with him. They're wearing ski jackets and sunglasses, but I know it's them. Hurry! He's got a gun!" I screeched.

"Okay, I'm sending out some cars, and I'm coming too. Which entrance?"

"The one in the middle across from the big parking garage... near Nordstrom's... there's a North Face store right next to the door," I panted as I ran down the sidewalk. "But, they just ran out and went into the parking garage."

"Listen, Jenny, don't try to follow them. It's too dangerous. Stay put and I'll call you when we get there."

"What? No! I can't let him take her out of here. He might kill her!"

"No," he said, "I'm *serious*. Stay put!"

Without answering him, I hung up and took off after the pair. I huffed, looking both ways before I dashed across the narrow street between the mall and the garage.

The man and Callie ran up the flight of stairs near the garage entrance. I followed, breaking into a full sprint.

They ran to a mid-size gray sedan and got in. They were maybe a hundred yards ahead of me. I couldn't let them leave.

The car backed up and screeched past me. The man stuck the gun out his rolled-down window and fired a shot. The last thing I saw before I went down was Callie's tear-streaked and panicked face plastered against the back window of the sedan.

Chapter 14

Haze.

Beeping.

Antiseptic.

My eyes opened a crack.

Oh God… not the hospital again. What happened?

"Jenny?"

A face hovered over me. It was Dr. Williams.

Detective Coalfield stepped into view.

"Detective?" I asked numbly, "What happened?"

"You were shot, but luckily, the bullet just grazed your temple. I rode in the ambulance with you," he said, his face a mask of anguish. "You could have died! I told you not to follow them!"

"I'm sorry," I said defiantly. "But I couldn't just let that creep take her. I *needed* to stop him."

He shook his head, clearly disappointed in me.

I sighed. "I guess I didn't do such a good job, huh?"

"You're a kid," he said simply. "There was nothing you could have done to stop him. The guy had a gun."

"What happened?" I asked. "I remember the man driving off with Callie, but I don't know what happened after that. I must have passed out."

"He shot you," he said weakly, "And he was aiming to kill. The bullet grazed your temple. We found it next to the staircase. The lab is doing an analysis on it. I still can't believe you ran after them!"

"It's okay. I'm not really hurt. But I wasn't going to stand by and do nothing," I said. And it was true. I didn't think I could've let that man take Callie away without trying to follow them.

"Can you describe him for me? And maybe give a description of his car?"

"I'll try. He was pretty covered up." I gave him the best description I could and he jotted everything down in his notebook.

"Now, how did you meet up with them in the first place?" he asked. "It blows my mind that he took his victim to the mall, of all places."

"I was shopping for an audition outfit. I saw two people on the other side of the store. They were wearing parkas, baseball caps, and sunglasses. But the really weird thing is, he pulled her over to the security camera, took off her cap and glasses and let the camera get a full view of her."

"What?" he asked in disbelief.

"Yeah, I know! Why would he do that?"

He thought for a moment and then answered, "Because he wanted us to know he had her, and that she was still alive."

"Whoa. Couldn't he have just let her talk on the phone to the police or her parents? Why did he bring her out in public? Seems too risky to me."

"Because he's a smug bastard. He was showing off. Some criminals are like that. They like to think they are more clever than the police," he answered wryly.

I winced as the doctor cleaned the side my face with alcohol. He patted it dry and covered the wound with a bandage.

"Your parents are on their way over here," Dr. Williams said. "But don't worry, you are just fine. We've already checked you out. You can go home as soon as they get here."

He walked toward the door. "This is the last time I want to see you here, okay?"

"Oh God," I said realizing the impact of Dr. Williams' words. "I don't know what's worse… getting shot or explaining all of this to my parents."

"Well if anyone should be doing any explaining, it's me," Detective Coalfield said guiltily. "How could I let their precious seventeen-year-old girl go chasing after a kidnapper?"

"I defied *you*! I was the one who chose to chase after them. Okay? So enough self-pity from you!" I shouted, surprising not only him, but myself. "I'm the one who has to explain to my parents why I am in this situation in the first place!"

"What?" he asked, shocked at my outburst.

"I have to explain to my parents that I'm psychic."

There was a long moment of silence.

"You mean… they don't know?" he asked, his eyebrows raised.

"Nope. I told you, nobody knows." I looked down at my hands.

"How could that be?" he asked. "How is it possible to hide such a thing?"

"I guess I'm a good actress?" I said with a little laugh. "I don't know. I think my dad has no clue whatsoever. Mom—I think she knew at some point, but then I got so good at hiding it that she gladly forgot about it. I think it would freak her out."

"I see."

"What am I going to tell them?"

"The truth," he said simply.

I internalized that for a moment. The truth. It sounded so simple, but I could think of a dozen reasons why it wasn't. Before I could think about how I would tell them or what I would say, my parents rushed through the door.

"Jenny!" my mom flew across the room and grabbed my arm. "What happened? They told us you'd been shot!"

I looked at Detective Coalfield standing by the window and swallowed hard.

My dad went to the other side of my bed and held my hand, his expectant face turned toward me.

"Uh... I was at the mall. I drove there—I wanted to test out my driving skills again."

Mom squeezed my hand, encouraging me to go on.

"I was in J. Crew and I was looking for an outfit for the audition. I saw Callie. You know, the missing girl?"

My dad looked puzzled. "You mean she was there, shopping?"

"Yes, well, no. Not exactly. She was disguised and there was a man with her; a man with a gun."

"What?" my mom asked incredulously.

"I know, it sounds weird, but she looked at me, and the man—well, he saw that I noticed them."

"And then?" my dad asked.

I hesitated. "And then they ran."

Mom squinted her eyes at me, suspiciously.

I looked down at my hands. "And I ran after them."

"You what?"

I crossed my arms. "What was I supposed to do? Let that monster take off with Callie? I had to see if I could stop him!"

My dad looked stunned and my mom looked angry.

"I can't believe..."

But she was cut short when Detective Coalfield stepped in.

"I told her to not to follow them," he said. He looked at my dad. "I'm sorry, Mr. Crumb. Jenny called me and told me she saw Callie and her kidnapper and I told her to stay put, but she..."

My mom looked at him like he was crazy. "What? Why did she call you? Why not call 911?" She turned to look at me. "He had a gun! He could've killed you!"

"I know. It was stupid. But I just couldn't let him take her."

"You two seem to know each other better than I would have expected," my dad interrupted. "Jenny, what's this all about? Why did you call Detective Coalfield directly instead of 911?"

"Mom… Dad," I broke in. "I was helping Detective Coalfield on this case. It was my decision to run after them. The thought of this guy getting away with Callie—I just couldn't let that happen."

"Whoa! Wait a minute!" My dad said. "Back up. You said you were helping on this case? That's crazy! Teenage girls do *not* help the police with kidnapping cases, or any cases for that matter! What is the meaning of this?" He glared at the detective.

I looked at Detective Coalfield and held his gaze for a moment. He gave me a nod that seemed to say, go on.

"The reason I was helping him on the case is because …" I took a deep breath. "It's because I'm psychic."

The words hung in the air.

My parents' eyes widened.

"What?" my mom said, flustered.

"I'm psychic," I continued a little more bravely.

"Oh come on, that's ridiculous!" my dad boomed. "If you were psychic, don't you think we would have known it?"

My mom let out a sigh. "I thought you were… when you were little," she confessed.

My dad shot a confused look at my mom. "What? You never told me…"

"I know, I know," Mom admitted. "She predicted my dad's death. I kept it quiet, hoping that it would go away. And it did." She looked at me. "At least, I thought it did."

"Well, it didn't," I answered. "I saw the look you gave me when you realized that I had predicted Grandpa's death. I scared you. I didn't like that. I didn't want my own mother to be scared of me."

Tears gathered in my mom's blue eyes. "You were hiding it from me? All these years?"

I hoped she wasn't too hurt that I'd kept my secret from her. I thought I was doing her a favor. Now I realized that it had only delayed the worry and made her feel bad.

"A four-year-old... protecting her mother? To keep her from being afraid? What kind of mother am I? The kind of mother a little girl feels like *she* has to protect?"

"Mom, I love you," I said. "I didn't want you to be scared. I could tell that it bothered you. I just thought life would be easier if you didn't have to deal with something that scared you. That's all."

She reached over and hugged me. "That's very selfless of you, Jenny," she sniffed. "But, I could've handled it. I could've helped you a little."

"How? How could you have helped me?" I asked.

"Well, I've had a few experiences like you've had," she said. "Not very many, but the things I saw scared me. A lot."

I looked at her incredulously. "You? You are psychic?"

"No—well, maybe a little. I pretty much suppressed it. It *did* scare me. I didn't like it, so I ignored it and eventually, it faded."

Whoa. My mom was psychic. Trippy.

"Mary?" My dad looked crushed. "You never told me."

She shook her head. "I thought I'd lose you if you knew."

"Are you kidding me?" My dad went over to my mom's side of the bed. He hugged her and tilted her face up to his.

"I wouldn't care if you were a witch doctor and practiced voodoo all day! I *love* you," he whispered and then kissed her.

"Ewww! Get a room. That's gross!" I hid my eyes.

The tension in the room broke and everyone laughed.

A nurse poked her head in the door. "Hey, the media is out here. They want to talk to Jenny," she said.

I tensed.

Detective Coalfield shook his head and held up a hand. "No, I'll talk to them in a minute. They need to leave Jenny out of this."

She shrugged and closed the door. I let out a sigh of relief.

"Thanks, Detective," I said gratefully.

"No problem," he answered. "The last thing I want to do is to have you surrounded by the media. Not only would it be bad for you, but it could also jeopardize our finding Callie."

The thought of being hounded by cameras gave me the creeps. If they found out the shooting was linked to Callie's disappearance, and then linked it to me... I just couldn't imagine what would happen.

Chapter 15

Audition day.

I was nervous, but I tried to get it out of my mind. I got up extra early, got out the white candle and did my morning meditation. Mom had gone to the mall after I had come back from the hospital and picked up the sweater that I wanted at J. Crew, so I slipped that on with a pair of jeans. I combed my hair over the graze on my temple. No sense in drawing attention to my injury.

At school, I sat through first period, not even really listening to what the teacher had to say. I asked to use the hall pass to go to the bathroom.

The halls were quiet. Only a dull murmur could be heard from within the closed classrooms. As I turned the corner, the girl, or rather, ghost that I had met before, was walking toward me. I stopped. Who is this girl? I wondered. So, I asked.

"Hi!" I said, maybe too cheerfully.

"Hello," she said quietly. "Have you seen my boyfriend?"

"Uh, no I haven't. Sorry," I said. "What's your name?"

"Michelle," she said simply. "I can't find my boyfriend. I know he must be here somewhere."

On a hunch, I asked her, "Michelle, what year is it?"

She gave me a funny look. "It's 1979. Why did you ask me that?"

"I was just confused for a second," I answered.

She frowned. "Well, if you see him, will you tell him that I'm looking for him?"

"Sure, I'll tell him," I answered. And with that, she disappeared.

Chills ran down my spine again. Would I ever get used to that?

In the bathroom, I thought... 1979. Huh. I think my mom and dad graduated in 1979. Mom went to Newport High. I made a mental note to ask her about Michelle and her boyfriend, John Cook.

***

The day passed quickly. I had butterflies, or at least caterpillars, in my stomach all afternoon. It was 2:45 p.m., and auditions started in fifteen minutes. I put my backpack in my locker and took out my sheet music. I walked down the narrow hallway to the Commons. The place was packed. It seemed as though a hundred or more students gathered in the area around the tables and chairs. A long table was set up with students manning the registration lists. I stood in line and waited to fill out the paperwork. A few minutes later, I was at the front of the line and filling out my form. Someone tapped me on the shoulder, and I turned to see who it was.

"Hey!" Madeline laughed. She was standing right behind me. "I was wondering how long it would take you to notice I was right behind you!"

I slapped my hand on my forehead. "Doh! I guess I was too nervous to notice anyone else."

I waited for her to fill out her form and then we stood watching the door at the top of the steps that led to the auditorium. A chubby theatre kid with a goatee, mustache, and glasses held a clipboard and checked his watch. He turned and went down the hall to the auditorium doors, yelled something and then reappeared at the top of the stairs.

"Okay! Listen up people," he shouted down at us. "We are about to begin. I will call your name according to the order on the sign-up sheet."

"Oh God," I said nervously, wiping my sweaty palms on my jeans.

"Yeah, I know. I'm kind of nervous too," Madeline confessed. "My time slot is 3:10–you're right after me, right?"

"Yup."

"We can do this!" she said, looking as if she was trying to convince herself just as much as she was trying to convince me.

I took a deep breath. In my head I thought, 'Let the white light of the holy spirit surround and protect me.' Oh brother. Did I really think God and the angels would get me through *this*? What the heck, it was worth a shot. It certainly couldn't hurt to say a little prayer before I went on stage.

The chubby kid yelled down, "I'm calling two of you up at a time! First up, Leah Mahoney and Mike Kramer!"

A short girl with dark curly hair straightened her shirt, stood up, and pushed her chair back. A guy a little further away from Leah stood up and grabbed his music. He was tall, had medium brown hair, and green eyes. I couldn't take my eyes off of him.

He was the guy who had asked Julia and me where his classroom was earlier in the year. "Who is that?" I whispered to Madeline.

"Oh—that's Mike Kramer. Didn't you hear his name being called? He's new. I think he's a senior."

We watched as they walked up the stairs and disappeared down the hall. The doors closed.

Ten minutes later, the chubby guy reappeared. "Okay! Next up, Madeline Coalfield and Jenny Crumb!"

108

The other students turned to stare at us. I could hear people whispering, "Isn't she a cheerleader? What is she doing here?"

I swallowed hard.

"What happened to Leah and Mike?" I whispered to Madeline as we ascended the stairs. "Why didn't they come out?"

"They probably went out the other doors near the stage," she whispered back.

We opened the doors at the end of the hall into the auditorium. The stage was down at the bottom and four people sat in the fourth row with clipboards in their laps. The chubby guy took our forms to them and told us to give the accompanist our music when we got up on stage.

Madeline worked her way down to the stage, climbed up the steps, and handed over her music. I sat in the back and slumped down in a chair, not wanting to make her more nervous by being conspicuous.

She stood stage center and looked at the directors. "I'm Madeline Coalfield and I'm a sophomore. I'll be doing a monologue from *Anne of Green Gables* and singing *My New Philosophy* from *You're a Good Man Charlie Brown*."

Wow, she sounded so confident.

The directors nodded for her to go ahead.

Watching her during her monologue, I forgot that she was a sophomore at Newport High School and fully believed she was Anne. Her mannerisms changed, the way her speech flowed… it was all different from the real Madeline. Amazing. I was mesmerized.

Next, she became Sally from Charlie Brown. Quippy, precocious Sally. She was so good! I felt bad when a pang of jealousy seared through me. Is this how wannabe cheerleaders felt during try-outs when they watched me go ahead of them? As jealous as I was, I was grateful for her friendship. I was grateful that she worked with me and

109

shared tips to make me better for this audition. And I was proud of her.

Madeline's song ended.

"Next!" the chubby boy yelled up to me.

Madeline walked out to the exit, but I could see her peeking through the door, which was slightly ajar. She gave me a thumbs up.

My legs felt rubbery as I walked down the steps toward the stage. I walked up the short flight of stairs and handed my music to the piano player.

"My name is Jenny Crumb. I'm a junior," I said quickly.

"Speak up!" yelled one of the directors. Oh God. I cleared my throat and tried again.

"My name is Jenny Crumb. I'm a junior," I said louder and more slowly. "I'll be doing a monologue from *One Minute Monologues for Teens,* and singing *Reflection* from *Mulan*," I said.

Was this a real moment or a dream? It was almost like an out-of-body experience—like I was watching someone else on stage. I had rehearsed the monologue and music so many times. Now was the time to make all the rehearsals pay off. I took a deep breath and began.

When I finished, I looked down at the directors. They smiled. One of them said, "Good! Go on."

I glanced at the accompanist and she motioned for me to begin the song.

The anxious girl who was hiding her psychic ability from everyone was gone. I was the girl in *Mulan* singing to her reflection in the water. My insecurities left me and I sang. I just sang out her feelings and her wish to discover who she really was.

When I finished, I looked down at the directors again.

They looked pleased. I least, I thought they did. Some of them were nodding and writing notes on their forms.

"Thank you!" one of them called.

I waved and left the stage and went out the exit doors. Madeline ambushed me with a big hug.

"You were fantastic!" she said breathlessly. "You are SO getting a part!"

"Thanks! You were great too! I bet the directors were blown away by you. I sure was." A mixture of relief and euphoria washed over me. "What an adrenaline rush!"

"No kidding," she said, still grinning. "Come on— let's go to get a bite to eat to celebrate."

***

"So, who were the directors and how does this whole audition process work?" I munched on a gyro at the Greek deli in the mall.

Madeline finished chewing and said, "Well, the one on the left was Mr. Jackson. He's the musical director for the drama department. The lady with the blond hair next to him is Ms. Farber. She's the assistant director. Then there's Ms. Nakamura—she's the director. And last but not least, is Mr. Weinhold. He's the stage manager."

"So when they're all finished with the auditions, what do they do?" I took a sip of my iced tea.

"They get together and start sorting through the forms. They throw out the ones that were terrible. Then, they separate those who were exceptional from those that were pretty good."

"But how do they decide who is right for what role?"

"First, there are callbacks. That's when you get called back because the director thinks that you could be right for a part. They have you read for different characters, and that helps them to figure out who is better for certain roles. That's my favorite part because it's not as scary as the initial audition. It's fun because you get to try on different characters and you're reading with a bunch of other people."

I shrugged. "Hmmm, interesting."

"I wouldn't want their job," Madeline admitted. "That's a lot of pressure deciding who will play what role."

"No kidding," I agreed. "So, when do we find out if we got a part?"

"They'll post callback results on the wall outside the auditorium at 2:30 tomorrow," she said. "I think callbacks are Wednesday after school."

My cell phone rang in my pocket. "Hello?"

"Jenny, it's Detective Coalfield."

"Oh, hi! I'm just sitting here with your daughter," I said. Madeline looked up from her plate.

"Tell her hello from her old dad," he said.

"Okay, I'll do that. What's up?"

"The Shoemakers have gotten a call from the kidnapper," he said. "We recorded it and I'd like you to come over to our house to listen to it before you go home."

Chapter 16

The voice changer made his voice sound like it was recorded in slow motion—unnaturally deep and strange. The hair on the back of my neck stood up as I listened to Detective Coalfield's flash recorder.

I was alone in the room with the Detective. Madeline didn't want to listen. She was afraid of losing it if she heard the voice of Callie's kidnapper. I didn't blame her.

"Do you have the money?" the voice asked.

"Not quite yet, we have most of it," Callie's dad answered, his voice quivering a little.

"When can you have the rest?" the kidnapper purred.

"I don't know, we are trying really hard … it's been difficult."

"Well, that's too bad. I guess I'll get to play with your daughter a little longer," he said, sounding amused. He was toying with them, like a cat playing with a mouse before he inflicted the fatal blow.

"You monster!" Callie's dad yelled in outrage.

"Shhh! Shhh!" Callie's mom hushed in the background. "Shhh! Don't."

The deep voice chortled. "Aww, what a protective daddy you are. Don't you feel helpless? Powerless? You should … because I'm the one in control now."

Callie's dad was silent now.

"Come up with the rest of the money. In the meantime, I'll get to spend more quality time with your daughter—right, Callie?"

I heard a scuffle on the recorder, like he had grabbed Callie and thrust her over near the phone.

"Right," she said meekly.

"Callie!" her dad cried out.

"Daddy!" her mournful voice echoed back.

Then, a dial tone.

"Oh God," I moaned. "We've got to find her!"

"There is a glimmer of good news in that recording. He hasn't threatened to kill her if they don't come up with the money right away." The detective shifted in his chair.

"Yeah, but what's better? Being tortured for an indefinite amount of time or killed? I think I'd choose the latter." I sucked in a breath, nearly in tears.

"We can't think about that," Detective Coalfield said. "We have to focus on finding her and getting her back alive." He paused. "You know, this guy seems to take great pleasure in tormenting Callie's father. That almost makes me wonder if he knows him. Maybe he's getting back at him for something. Can you try focusing your attention on that possibility?"

I shrugged. "I can try, but I don't know how much control I've got. I don't think I can direct what images I get."

"Well, just do your best. Give it a try as soon as you can." He left the rest unspoken, but I knew what he was saying. Try to find her, so Callie wouldn't have to endure any more of this nightmare than she had to.

***

After I got home, I got the white candle from the mantel and went to my room. The house was quiet. Jackson was at his friend's house and mom and dad were

114

still at work. I sat cross-legged on the floor of my room and lit the candle. I closed my eyes and took in deep breaths, releasing the air slowly and purposefully.

"Let the light that gives light to the universe enter all my being," I chanted. "Let the light that gives light to the universe enter all my being, Let the light that gives light to the universe enter all my being," I kept chanting until I felt a calm inner peace come over me.

"God? Spirit? Angels?"

How was I supposed to do this? I felt awkward as I searched for a poetic way to talk to my higher power.

"Umm, I need help." I stumbled over the words. "Please help me to see who Callie's kidnapper is. Help me to find out if he has a connection to Callie's father or family… help me to find out where she is so we can rescue her."

Nothing.

"Are you there?"

I was interrupted by the call of an eagle. Huh? I heard it again—louder this time. I jumped up, nearly tripping over the candle, hopped onto my bed and looked out my window.

A bald eagle soared over the treetops, calling its beautiful, but eerie cry.

That was weird. I knew that bald eagles had taken up residence over by Lake Washington. I had seen many of them at Newcastle Beach Park. But I hadn't seen many in my neighborhood. What did that mean? Did it mean anything at all? What did a bald eagle have to do with Callie's kidnapper and his connection to her dad? Or did it have something to do with where Callie was being held captive?

Maybe nothing.

I tried again, repeating my mantra sitting with the candle.

Nothing. Nothing at all.

I blew out the candle, took it downstairs and returned it to the fireplace mantel. I called Detective Coalfield and told him about the eagle.

"An eagle, huh?" he said, puzzled. "That could mean lots of things, I suppose."

"Or nothing," I replied quietly.

"Or nothing," he repeated. "Maybe you could try again later," he added.

"I'll keep trying." I felt so dejected. This was life or death for Callie. I needed to come through for her.

Chapter 17

My last class of the day was Physics. I was surprised that the experiment my team was working on didn't collapse. My head was just not in it. All I could focus on was the callback list being posted at 2:30 p.m.

"Jenny!" shouted Chris Buehler, who was unfortunately not only in my Anatomy and Physiology class, but also in my Physics class. "Watch what you're doing! You almost knocked the whole thing over!"

I jerked back from the contraption we were building. "Sorry," I said as my face burned red. "Somebody else better do this, I'm not very effective today."

Chris glared at me. "I thought you weren't a cheerleader anymore, but you sure act like you are."

"I said I was sorry." I glared back, but I realized that he was right. Cheerleaders could get away with not paying attention in class. Most guys were quick to help out a cheerleader, just so they could try to ask them out later. There were definite benefits to belonging to that kind of crowd. Truthfully, I was competent enough in my own class work—I didn't need any guy's help, and I had never tried to take advantage of them. But just this once, it would have been nice for someone else to step in and help me, because I simply could not concentrate.

Mr. Owen stood up from behind his desk.

"Okay, class—time's up. I'm coming around to check each group's work and then you can clean up and head out."

There was a collective groan in the classroom as most teams had not accomplished the goal that Mr. Owen had set for us.

After we had cleaned up our work area, I slung my backpack over my left shoulder and stepped into the hallway. The sea of students swallowed me up and carried me through the halls with the tide. The architect who designed the school used to design prisons—and I was sure he had forgotten that his plans were for a school and not a penitentiary. The openings from hallway to hallway were impossibly narrow, so that there was always a big bottleneck at the end.

I struggled to veer off course, fighting like a salmon going upstream, and angled through the hallway near the drama department. A group of anxious-looking teens were gathered around the list. I stopped, watching in fascination as one by one, their faces lit up or fell, depending on the outcome written on the wall.

If it was good news, they shouted, "I made it through!" But if it was bad news, they hid their faces and slunk off, sometimes being consoled by their friends.

My stomach churned. What if I didn't get called back? What if I did? Both options seemed frightening.

I caught a glimpse of Madeline in between some taller girls. I waved.

She caught sight of me. "Hi!" she called to me. "Come over here!"

I edged through some of the disappointed people who were leaving the hallway and slipped in beside her.

"Do you know yet?" I asked.

"Nope," she said cheerfully. "Let's look together." She grabbed my hand and pulled me over to the list. I felt sick with anxiety. Her name was first. She was called back. My name was underneath hers…

"Yes!" I screamed and hugged her.

We jumped up and down, giggling. Some of the other students laughed and nudged each other. Others glared and walked away—sore losers, I guessed.

As we were turning to leave the hallway, I bumped right into the new guy, Mike Kramer. My face slammed right into his chest. He was tall. I looked up, my face burning red for the second time that day.

"Oh God! I'm sorry!" I stuttered.

He looked down at me, his green eyes shining in amusement. "No problem."

A slight smile crept to the corner of his mouth and then he made his way to the list. Green. That was my new favorite color.

Madeline and I watched his reaction to what he read. He looked pleased and then walked briskly past us.

Madeline looked at me curiously. "You like him, don't you?"

"Huh?" I asked, startled.

"Mike. You like the new guy, Mike." She smiled mischievously.

"What are you talking about?" I tried glossing it over. It didn't work.

"Ha!" Madeline crowed. "Maybe you'll get to kiss him in the play!" She elbowed me in the arm.

"Oh come on! Give me a break!"

We snickered and made our way to our lockers. My stomach fluttered. Maybe I *would* get to kiss him in the play.

Chapter 18

Madeline and I entered the theatre together. Callbacks would start in five minutes. I was nervous, but she was excited.

"This is going to be so much fun!" She beamed at me. "You're going to love it."

"How can you be so cheerful all the time?" I groaned. "This whole process has me all edgy."

"Snap out of it!" She giggled. "I'm telling you—this is fun."

I rolled my eyes and followed her to the rows halfway down the main aisle. The other kids were filing in and setting their stuff down on some of the seats. I looked around.

"Looking for someone in particular?" Madeline asked slyly.

"What? No! Of course not. I'm just checking out how many people are here," I said a little too quickly.

"Yeah, right."

"Shut up!"

Then I saw him. He was sitting in the fourth row up from the stage. He was staring intently at the black curtain, but then he must have felt me staring at him because he turned and looked right at me and a smile played across his lips. Not a big smile, just the corner of the mouth thing that he did when I bumped into him.

I quickly looked away, pretending to watch for someone walking down the stairs.

"Oooh, he's looking at you," Madeline teased. "Want me to go talk to him and see if he's interested?"

"No!" I said loudly. Some of the other kids near us, turned around and stared. "Don't you dare."

"Oh, okay. You big chicken."

The director walked up the stairs to the stage. The curtains opened and everyone was silent. "Hello, everyone! Congratulations for making it to callbacks. You are a very talented group of people."

Some of the students clapped each other on the backs.

"So, here is how the process works." Ms. Nakamura continued. "We are going to call groups of you onto the stage and have you read for different parts. You may only get to read for one part, or we may try you in several different parts and or several different groups."

"While one group is on stage, another will be back in the green room with our musical director, Mr. Jackson, working on songs. Or, you will have a turn out in the hall with the choreographer, working on some dance steps. You'll all get a chance to do all of those. Then in the last hour, we will bring you all together, and do a scene with a little music. Sound good?"

The audience murmured in acknowledgement. Several people whooped and clapped, ready to work.

"Good! Let me read out the names for each group."

Madeline was in Group A, in the green room with Mr. Jackson. I was assigned to Group B, on stage, reading, and Mike Kramer was assigned to Group C, in the hallway, learning dance steps. Damn.

I read for the Baker's Wife and Cinderella. Derek Barry, the guy Hannah had a crush on, read for the Baker and for Cinderella's prince. He was really good. I wondered if he could sing as well as he acted.

Next, I went into the hall with my group to do some dance steps. The choreographer, Ms. Walsh, taught us some simple dance steps and noted if we caught on quickly or not, writing on her clipboard. It felt weird being judged on every move I made. I had this one in the bag, though. Years of cheerleading had taught me coordination and how to catch on to new moves quickly.

Then, on to the green room to sing. There were lots of good singers in my group… and lots who were not. One girl, Amanda, was strangely confident, but couldn't match the pitch very well. I caught her glaring at me when I sang the part of the Baker's wife. Was I singing badly too?

Finally, we gathered together in the theatre to do a scene. They called different groups of people, randomly it seemed, to sing and read. Again, I read and sang for the part of the Baker's wife and Cinderella.

This time, instead of being paired with Derek Barry, I was paired with Mike Kramer and another guy, Scott Hames.

Scott was a pretty good singer. Mike was much better. I was drawn to him like a moth to a flame… and forgot who I was completely. Talk about chemistry. At least, *I* felt it. Did he? He was so professional on stage; I couldn't tell what he felt.

The director called out, "Good job, everyone! You are free to go home. Results will be posted tomorrow at 2:30 p.m., same place as the callbacks were posted."

Everyone gathered their stuff up from the seats and chatted as we exited the theatre.

"Did you have fun?" Madeline asked.

"Yeah, I did!" I said, thinking about Mike and his green eyes.

"Told ya." She winked at me.

Chapter 19

The next day should have crawled by as I waited for the results, but it didn't. I had a quiz in my U.S. History class and a test in my Spanish class. I had no time to lose focus over the callback results.

Finally, the last bell rang. I felt confident about the tests I took, but now my stomach turned to jelly. My nerves grabbed hold of me and caused an earthquake to vibrate through my body.

I fought my way to the hallway where the results would be posted and walked hurriedly to the list. I felt someone's hands on my arms from behind me. I thought at first that it was Madeline, but then I heard a masculine voice say, "You're shaking."

It was Mike.

Oh my God.

"Let's go find out what you got… it's Jenny, right?" he asked.

I was speechless.

He pushed me forward gently, until we were right in front of the list.

"Jenny Crumb…" he said as his finger followed the names down the list. "You got the Baker's Wife! That's a big part."

I didn't know if I was more stunned to find out that I got a big part or that he was speaking to me.

His finger kept going down the list. "Hey! I got the part of the Baker. Guess we're married!"

I felt like I was going to hurl. Too much excitement for one day.

"What's the matter? Aren't you happy with that part? Or is it that you don't want to be married to me?" His eyes twinkled in amusement.

"Uh…" God, I was so brilliant. All I could say was, 'Uh.'

Madeline rescued me. She came out of nowhere, grabbed my hand and squealed.

"Oh my God! You got the Baker's Wife and I got Little Red. Oh my God!" She grabbed my arms and laughed, but then stopped as she noticed Mike standing there.

"Oh," she said. "Sorry—didn't mean to interrupt."

He shook his head. "No, you weren't interrupting anything."

"Oh," she said again and looked at me apologetically.

I came out of my stupor. "Congratulations on your awesome role!"

"Thanks! Congrats to you too." She beamed. "What did you get, Mike?"

"I got the Baker," he answered smoothly.

"Oh," she said with a little sly grin. "Oh, yeah—wow! Congratulations!"

"Thanks," he said graciously.

We walked into the theatre to pick up our scripts, brushing by Amanda, who again scowled at me.

Madeline whispered to me, "Don't pay any attention to her. She's just mad because she got an ensemble part. She's jealous of you."

Mike glanced at Amanda. "She looks pretty mad. What did you do to her?"

"Nothing!" I said, giving him a sideways glance. "I've never even met her before. She was in my singing group during callbacks. That's the first time I ever saw her."

"She's a sophomore. She's been in a couple of productions here—even had kind of a big part, but no singing in that role," Madeline offered.

"She wasn't all that good during callbacks. Maybe she's upset because I got the role that she wanted? I don't know."

"Don't worry about her," Mike added. "She'll get over it."

Maybe she would, maybe she wouldn't.

We picked up our scripts. Ms. Nakamura was standing on stage. "First rehearsal starts tomorrow at 2:45. Bring a snack and a bottle of water. Oh, and read through your scripts!"

We walked out into the hall together.

"Well girls, see you tomorrow afternoon!" Mike winked and headed down the hall toward his locker.

"He is so into you!"

"He is not." I hid my smile. "Hey, want a ride home?"

"Sure! I'll go get my stuff."

She went to her locker way down at the other end of the hall, and I went to mine. As I got near it, Hannah, Julia, and Aya turned the corner toward me. Oh Lord.

I smiled tentatively at them. "Hi guys! Long time, no see."

"Hi!" they all chimed in, looking relieved.

"What are you still doing here?" Aya asked.

"I was picking up my script for the play."

"You got a part?" Hannah asked. "Congratulations!"

"Yeah, congratulations." Julia looked uncomfortable again. "Listen, Jenny." She stumbled over her words. "What I said a while back, about not being one of us anymore. I'm really sorry. I don't know what came over me. I'm just really, really sorry." She hung her head.

I reached out and grabbed her hand. "It's okay. I shouldn't have stormed off like that either. Friends?"

Her face brightened and she breathed a sigh of relief. "Yes! Friends!"

"Thank God." Hannah said. "I'm so glad you two finally came to your senses."

Just then, Madeline came down the hall with her backpack. I grabbed her by the shoulder. "Girls, I'd like you to meet my new friend, Madeline."

The girls paused a moment to check her out.

"She really helped me to get a part—she's a great coach," I said putting my arm around her.

"Oh—well, that's great!" Aya said. "Aren't you a sophomore?"

"Yes, I'm a sophomore," Madeline said.

"Hey, no class distinctions, girls! She's a good friend!"

"No worries," Hannah joked. "We won't hold it against her."

***

I dropped Madeline off at her house and drove home. When I opened the door, Mom, Dad, and Jackson were sitting at the table eating freshly baked chocolate chip cookies and had glasses of milk. The aroma was intoxicating.

"Hi!" Mom said as she handed me a cookie and a glass of milk.

"Wow! What's the occasion?" I asked, taking a bite of the warm, chewy, goodness.

"Isn't today the day that you find out about the play?" Mom asked.

"Well?" my dad asked anxiously.

"Well, I'm sorry to say…" I hung my head down and tried not to smile.

My parents moved closer to me, expecting me to need them for comfort.

I looked up. "I got the part of the baker's wife!"

Mom and Dad threw their arms around me, laughing.

"Congratulations, sweetie!" Dad said, kissing my cheek.

"Woohoo," Jackson said nonchalantly. "The baker's wife. Big deal. You'll probably get like one or two lines. Like, 'I'll make some bread' or, 'let me start the oven.'"

"Hey!" Mom said sharply. "You could at least be happy for her."

"By the way," I said directly to Jackson, "The baker's wife is one of the biggest roles in the musical."

"It is?" Dad asked.

"Believe it or not—it is."

Jackson shrugged. "Whatever."

***

After dinner and homework, I grabbed the candle off the mantelpiece and took it upstairs to my room. I changed into my pajamas, brushed my teeth and sat on the floor with the candle.

I sat for a long while with the candle glowing, trying to still my mind. Once I had driven all the random thoughts from my brain, I thanked God, the universe, and anyone else who might be listening for helping me to get my role in the play. Then I said thanks for my wonderful family and friends. Even Jackson was mentioned, begrudgingly.

Now on to the next task… asking for help with Callie.

"I need your guidance and counsel," I asked. "I need to know if there is a connection between Callie's kidnapper and her family. Why did this man take *her*?"

I waited.

I tried again. "Help me find out who this man is and where to find Callie."

I waited.

"Help me to…" I stopped. Through my closed eyelids, the light of the candle had wavered. I opened my eyes. The candle flame flickered wildly.

"Uh oh," I said to myself. "Here we go."

Before me, at eye level, I saw a barrage of images coming in rapid succession.

Eagles, boats, small town, gray skies, Callie as a young girl, her father.

Stop.

Wait. Was that where Callie was now? But she was little in those images. Her father… did her father do this? Did he set this whole thing up? If that were true, then why? What motive did he have?

The candle flame flickered wildly, turning from yellow, to orange, to an angry red.

I saw the man.

He was standing behind Callie, holding her with his arms wrapped around her. His face was sweaty and flushed. Her face was set in a mask of repulsion. Tears flowed silently down her cheek.

"Well, my dear," he whispered into her ear. "It was fun talking to your parents. They weren't very helpful, were they? Oh well. Shall we go play?"

The candle went out abruptly.

I scrambled up from my position on the floor and grabbed my cell phone from the dresser and called Madeline's dad.

"This is Detective Coalfield."

"Oh my God! Detective, I saw something."

"Okay, Jenny, slow down. What did you see?"

I explained everything to him. The silence on the other end of the phone line was deafening.

128

"Detective?"

"I'm here," he answered. "Sorry, I was just thinking. I'm not a psychic, but I definitely get a sense that this guy knows Callie's dad."

"Really? You don't think that Callie's dad is part of this whole thing, is he? Do you think he set it up?"

"I don't think so. I don't know. But the way this guy seems to be toying with her dad—and hurting her. It could be revenge."

I wondered if we'd ever get to the bottom of this. It was so frustrating to get only little bits and pieces of information. I wanted to find out everything in one shot. Guess it didn't work that way.

"I'm going to interview Callie's parents again. I want to find out more about where they lived before they moved here and if they know anyone who might have it in for them," he said.

"Good luck," I answered. "I hope you find out some new information that will help."

"Okay, Jenny. Thanks for calling. I think this is a really good lead."

"Good, I hope it helps. Bye."

As I put my phone back down on the dresser, I couldn't help but wonder how much more of this Callie could take.

Chapter 20

The first rehearsal for the play started in fifteen minutes. I had a lot of nervous energy coursing through me. This was the beginning of my high school drama career. I hummed as I turned the combination lock, 1-right, 10-left, 6-right. Click.

My mind wandered as I transferred unneeded books into my locker. Did Mike really like me, or was I just imagining it?

"Boo!" An arm snaked around my shoulders, whirling me around.

"Oh!" I yelled a little too loudly. Aya, Julia, and Hannah had snuck up on me.

"You're a little jumpy, aren't you?" Julia asked.

"Yeah, who knew you were so skittish?" Hannah added.

"Yeah, well, who knew you guys were going to scare the crap out of me?"

"So, we were thinking," Aya said.

"We thought it would be fun to have a sleepover. Like old times!" Julia gushed.

Hannah grabbed my hand. "Come on—it will be fun."

I was surprised and glad that they were including me on a group event. "That sounds fun. I'll check with my parents before rehearsal. Do you want to do this tonight or tomorrow night?"

"How about tonight? Say around 7:00? When do you get out of rehearsal?" asked Julia. "We'll make dinner together."

"I'll be done by 6:00. That should give me enough time to go home and pack my stuff," I answered.

"Call them," urged Aya. "It'll be at my house."

Aya had a pretty big house with a downstairs that had a separate kitchen. We had the whole area to ourselves and could be as loud and obnoxious as we wanted.

I took out my cell phone and called my mom. I quickly asked her if I could go and she immediately agreed, delighted that I was back in with my old friends.

"Okay, I'm in," I said as I finished the call.

"Great!" said Julia. "We're going to the store and get the stuff for dinner. Anything special that you want? Tacos or spaghetti?"

"Tacos sound good. And don't forget the ice cream," I said.

"Tacos and ice cream it is, then," Hannah said. "Good luck at rehearsal!"

"Thanks," I said, closing my locker. "See you at 7:00."

***

People straggled into the auditorium. The adults gathered around the piano with sheet music and scripts, discussing their plan of attack for the first get-together.

I scanned the people who were already sitting in some seats near the stage. Madeline was there, sitting six rows back, rummaging through her backpack. I walked down the aisle and slipped into the seat beside her.

She looked up, surprised. "Hey!"

"Hey," I said, smiling.

She pulled out two protein bars from her pack. "Want one?"

"Sure. I brought some extra tangerines, if you want one."

"I love tangerines, but it looks like they are getting ready to start, so wolf that down."

I opened the wrapper and started chewing while Ms. Nakamura walked up the stairs to the stage.

"Congratulations on winning your roles in this production of *Into the Woods*. I am so happy to have such a wonderful and talented group of people here to work with."

All of us sitting in the audience chairs clapped and hooted.

"Today, we are going to do a read-through," Ms. Nakamura continued. "For those of you who don't know what that is, we sit in a circle on the stage and read through the script. You will obviously be reading for the role that you've been assigned in the play.

"So, let's start the reading and I'll play the CD throughout so we can listen to how the music fits into the play. We'll get a good sense of what it's all supposed to sound like. Okay?"

"Yeah!" A guy from the first row shouted, pumping his fist.

"Great! Everyone up on stage and sit in a tight circle please." She clapped her hands, encouraging us to move quickly.

I bumped into Amanda on my way up to the stage. Images flashed in front of me.

"You're not good enough to get a part like that!" her mom shouted at her. "You're too fat and ugly. If you get some of that pudge off of you, maybe you'd get a better role."

Whoa, now I felt sorry for the girl. I grabbed her arm and she turned to look at me angrily.

"What's your problem?" She wrenched her arm away.

"Sorry, Amanda," I said. "I just wanted to tell you that you look really nice today, and congratulations on getting a role. Great job!"

Her brow furrowed in confusion. "Thanks," she said awkwardly. I saw a hint of a smile on her lips. Maybe this gift wasn't so bad after all.

Madeline and I found a place in the circle and sat down.

There was a spot open on my left and someone sat down while I was whispering with Madeline.

It was Mike.

"I thought I should sit next to my wife," he said as he made himself comfortable, sitting cross-legged. "Any objections?"

"Ah, no. No objections."

I was already a little nervous for the read-through, but now my adrenaline kicked it up a notch or two. I took a swig from my bottle of water and tried to work out my jitters.

***

Somehow, we got through the read-through and I survived it. The easy part was listening to the CD. Mr. Jackson, the musical director, handed out our music so we could follow along with the music.

The listening part was a lot less stressful, but I sensed the electricity between Mike and I. Literally, I felt tingling in my left arm—which was the arm closest to him. He must have felt it too, because out of the corner of my eye, I caught him glancing at me now and then.

When we finally got up out of our circle on the stage, he touched my shoulder and turned me toward him. "The music is good, isn't it?" he asked.

"Yeah, it's really good."

He said looking into my eyes, "I am looking forward to Monday's rehearsal."

His green eyes were so luminescent… I couldn't pull my gaze away from them. In fact, I couldn't even move for a second. He smiled, enjoying the realization that he was having some sort of effect on me.

Madeline tapped me on the shoulder. "Hey, I wanted you to meet some of our cast mates. You've introduced me to your friends, so how 'bout if I introduce you to some of mine?"

I looked back reluctantly as Madeline grabbed my arm and tugged me away. Mike waved as he jumped off the stage and walked to the side exit.

"Sophia! Shannon! Ashley! Renee!" she called as she pulled me towards a small group of girls talking on stage. "I'd like you to meet my new friend, Jenny Crumb."

The four girls stopped chatting and looked me over curiously.

"Hi," Shannon said. "I saw you at callbacks—you were really great!"

"Thanks, so were all of you."

"Are they letting you out of cheerleading practice to do the play?" Ashley asked.

"Actually, no." I said. "I haven't been a cheerleader since I had that accident after the championship basketball game. I'm not allowed to cheer anymore."

Renee chimed in. "I heard about that. I didn't go to the game that night, but everyone was talking about it. Are you okay now?"

"Yes, I'm fine. I just have to be careful to not get too active or bump my head."

"That would be impossible for me." Renee said good-naturedly. "I seem to bump my head a lot. Being tall has its awkward disadvantages."

Sophia snorted. "Yeah, she actually just bumped her head on the stage when she jumped up here right before rehearsal."

Renee elbowed her with a grin. "Okay, short-stuff, that's enough."

"Well, I seem to being doing that a lot lately too. And I don't have the excuse of being tall." Madeline's friends were nice. It was good to meet people from outside my crowd for a change.

***

In the parking lot, I rummaged through my backpack to find my car keys. When I pulled them out, all the hairs on the back of my neck stood up.

Flash.

Someone was there ... a shape, crouching behind a red car dashed to another car nearby.

What the...? Someone tapped me on my right shoulder and I let out a shriek.

"Whoa! Jenny, it's okay, it's just me." Mike put his hands on my shoulders reassuringly.

"Don't scare me like that!"

"Uh, sorry, all I did was tap you on the shoulder."

"What do you mean? I saw you hiding behind that red car and then you hid behind another one." My heart pounded in my chest. "Are you trying to scare me to death? Because you were almost successful!"

"What? I wasn't hiding behind a car." He looked confused.

"Yes you were! I saw you!" I insisted. Wait a minute. I hadn't actually seen him hiding, I saw *someone* hiding. Or did I? Maybe what I saw was a premonition.

"Honestly," he said, putting his hand on my shoulder, "I wasn't hiding behind a car."

I looked into his gorgeous eyes and I could tell he was telling the truth.

I blinked.

"Well then, who was hiding back there?" I pointed to the red Toyota Camry.

"I don't know," he answered. "I didn't see anyone. Let's go have a look."

He took my backpack from me and slung it over his shoulder. We wove in and out of the parked cars and stopped momentarily to listen. Nothing.

"Huh," I shrugged. "I swear I saw someone crouching behind a car."

"Maybe your eyes were playing tricks on you," he said, smiling. He bent over and looked at me, not two inches away from my face. "But from what I can tell, your eyes are fine. In fact, they are the most beautiful shade of blue I have ever seen."

For a moment, I forgot to breathe.

I tore my gaze away and fought for composure as I felt my cheeks heat up. "You sure know how to sweet-talk a girl."

"Oh, I'm not sweet-talking you." He smiled that cute crooked smile. "It's the truth. Your eyes are beautiful—*you* are beautiful."

Oh my God.

He put his arm around me and walked me to my car. My heart was doing little flip-floppy hiccups in my chest. I didn't trust myself to speak, so I just unlocked my car door, my hands shaking. He went around the front of my car and opened the passenger door and for a moment, I thought he was going to get in. But then, he put my backpack on the seat, closed the door and came back around to my side.

"What are you doing this weekend?" he asked casually.

My mind raced. What was I doing this weekend? The word rolled around in my brain. Weekend, weekend, weekend. What was I doing this weekend?

I must have looked pretty funny during this exercise, because Mike grinned. The grin threw me out of my stupor.

"Sleepover!" I said triumphantly. I had regained control over my malfunctioning brain. Ha! I swear he had a virus-like effect on me, turning my brain into mush whenever he even looked at me.

"Sleepover?" he asked, surprised.

"Yeah, I'm hanging out with my friends—we're making tacos," I said.

"Tacos," he said, still grinning.

I raised my eyebrows. "Do you have a problem with tacos?"

He chuckled. "No, I don't. I just… never mind. What I was trying to do was ask you out." He looked down, suddenly uncertain of himself.

"Oh." My face flushed even more. "Well, I'd love that. I mean, I'd love to go out with you. But I've already made plans with my friends. I don't want to bail on them."

Why did the sleepover have to be this weekend?

"Sunday," he said.

"Sunday?"

"How about Sunday? For lunch. Say, noon?"

"Okay. Where?" My heart started doing the hiccup thing again.

"Something casual. Like Red Robin at Factoria Mall?" he asked.

"Yeah, okay, sure," I said a little too quickly.

His face lit up. "Okay then. It's a date."

A date.

Chapter 21

"We can play light as a feather, stiff as a board," Aya said.

"What?" I asked as I stuffed the last of my taco in my mouth.

"Oh, yeah," Julia said. "You know that good ol' classic sleepover game. Haven't you ever played it?" she asked as she went back for a second helping.

I shook my head. I'd never heard of it.

Hannah dabbed at her chin with a napkin. "Oh, I remember that one. We played it at Madison McCormick's sleepover in like, seventh grade. It was kind of creepy."

"Madison McCormick … do I know her?" I asked.

"She was only at our school for like six months or so," Aya answered. "I don't think you had any classes with her, so you probably wouldn't have known her."

"Anyway," Hannah added, "we played that game at her sleepover, and like I said, it's a little creepy."

"Creepy in what way?" I asked going back for my third helping of tacos.

"Well, it's just creepy. The way it works is that one person lies flat on her back on the floor. Then everyone else sits around the person."

"Then everyone puts their index fingers under the person who is lying on the floor," added Julia. "And, everyone starts chanting, 'light as a feather, stiff as a board' over and over again."

I shrugged. "Well … what's supposed to happen?"

"The person who is lying down is supposed to levitate—or something like that. The people who are lifting don't even feel her weight as they lift," Hannah explained.

My eyes widened. "Does that really work?"

"Yeah!" said Julia. "It worked at Madison's party. Then again, we had at least six or seven people lifting her."

"It probably wouldn't work then," I answered. "Because we only have the four of us—and one of us would be the person lying down. So we'd only have three people to lift. Seems impossible."

Julia giggled. "Well, what the heck, it will be fun to try!"

***

We finished scarfing down our tacos and cleaned up the kitchen.

"Should we try the game now?" Julia asked.

Hannah snickered. "After eating all those tacos, I don't think any of us will be light as a feather."

"Especially me. I think I ate four tacos," I joked.

"I hate that crazy metabolism of yours," Aya said. "You can eat anything and not gain weight."

"So," Hannah added, looking at me, "*you* should be the one that we lift!"

Oh brother.

I shrugged and said, "Suit yourselves. You'll never even get me an inch off the floor."

Aya ran upstairs to get some candles and I lay down on the floor with Julia on my left side and Hannah on my right. When Aya came back, she lit three candles and arranged them around us. Then she sat down behind on the left side with Julia.

"Okay. Shall we start?" she asked. "So, let's all take some deep breaths and close our eyes."

Julia giggled.

"No giggling," commanded Aya in her most serious tone.

Hannah snorted.

"No snorting either," Aya said. "Okay, breathe in… breathe out. Breathe in breathe out."

We spent about twenty seconds just breathing. My body started to relax.

"Now, everyone but Jenny repeat after me," Aya began. "Light as a feather, stiff as a board."

They began to chant with her. As they did, I must have gone into some kind of relaxed hypnotic state, because I couldn't hear them anymore.

Flash.

"No! I don't want to go back in there!" I cried, trying to fight the man.

"I told you," he hissed at me, pulling me by my arm, "until your parents can come up with the money, you need to stay underground."

"No!" I screamed.

"It's too risky keeping you in my house," he glared at me. "I can't watch you every second of the day. Someone might see you through the window or you might escape."

"I promise!" I insisted. "No one will see me… I won't try it."

"No," he said threateningly. "I can't trust you."

"But you can! I haven't tried to get away."

"You made eye contact with a person at the mall—you did that on purpose."

"But that wasn't my fault! I don't even know that girl!" I screamed.

"Oh, really," he said in a dangerously calm tone, "I think you do know her. She's beautiful… in fact, she's a lot prettier than you are. Tell me, what is her name?"

"I don't know her name," I said quietly.

He grabbed my arm and twisted it painfully behind my back. "I said, tell me her name."

"No," I winced.

"Tell... me... her... name," he said and pulled on my arm so hard, I heard a crack.

I screamed, "It's Jenny!"

"Jenny what?" he twisted harder and I could feel something loose in my arm come apart. Pain seared through me and spread like fire throughout my body.

"Crumb! Her name is Jenny Crumb!"

Thud. My back met the floor and rattled my bones.

A hush.

"Oh my God!" I heard Julia say. "Jenny?"

My eyes flew open, wide with terror.

Hannah shook me gently. "Jenny..."

Aya scooted around next to Hannah. "What happened? You screamed... what's going on?"

"He knows who I am!" I said with panic, trying to sit up. My arm hurt.

"What? Who?" Julia asked, looking shaken.

"The man! The man!" I squealed, my voice reaching a frenzied pitch.

"What man?" Hannah asked.

Before I even realized what it meant to reveal the answer, I blurted out, "The man who took Callie!"

Silence.

"The man... who took... Callie?" Aya asked with stunned disbelief. "How do you know that a man took Callie? What is this all about?"

I sighed.

Now I'd done it. The secret that I had kept for almost a lifetime was out. Just like that. I was sure that the walls would come tumbling down or that lightning would strike me.

More silence.

Hannah looked at me quizzically. "Jenny, I think you owe us some sort of explanation."

"I probably should have told you a long time ago," I admitted, guiltily.

"Tell us what?" Julia asked, leaning forward.

I grimaced, fearing a not-so-pleasant reaction.

"Tell you that I'm… psychic," I looked up at their faces expectantly.

"Psychic?" Hannah asked, surprised. "Oh come on! Psychic? I don't even believe there is such a thing!"

"I believe it," Julia said. "I do. I have an aunt who is like that. She never really talks about it, but she just seems to know stuff."

Hannah looked at her oddly. "Really? Come on! This is crap! Jenny, tell us what's really going on."

I looked down at my hands, embarrassed that Hannah thought I was lying.

"I'm telling the truth," I said. "Believe me; I never wanted to be psychic. It's not a joke, a game, or anything I'd ever choose for myself."

"Do you really expect us to believe this?" Hannah asked incredulously.

"I believe her," Aya said firmly. "Tell us more about it, Jenny."

I hesitated. "I've been this way ever since I can remember. I knew my grandfather had died before we got the official news. I knew things about people—like, if someone was sick or something was wrong with them. I just knew it."

"Okay, then, why haven't you told us? We've been friends for forever." Hannah demanded.

"Because it made me different from you guys. I didn't want to be a freak—the weird kid in school." I sighed.

"Okay, wait a minute. You are still assuming that we believe in this psychic stuff. I'm sorry, I just don't believe it! And if it's not real, then why are you telling us this?" Hannah sat back on her heels and crossed her arms.

Calm came over me. "Hannah, why don't you believe that some people are psychic? Are you scared of it?"

"No… well, not really. I've always thought it was just a bunch of bunk. You know, fortune tellers equal scam artists."

"Well, I can tell you for certain—it's real. It's very, very real," I said somberly.

"All right then—prove it," Hannah demanded.

"What?"

"I said, prove it." She glared at me.

I hesitated. "What would you like to know?" I asked.

"Tell me something about myself that nobody here knows," she said.

Aya gave her a wry look. "I don't think there's much we don't know about you. You're pretty much an open book."

"Well, I'm sure that there is *something* that she hasn't told us in there," I said.

I took Hannah's hand and held it. I closed my eyes.

Flash.

Hannah as a little girl, staring at a boy, a love-struck look on her face.

"In first grade, you liked Billy Mahoney," I said.

"Well, that's not news," Hannah snickered. "You guys probably all could've guessed that. Every girl in our class liked Bill Mahoney."

I kept my eyes closed.

"Okay, in third grade, the answers for the multiplication test were on your teacher's desk. The answer sheet was underneath a book, but was peeking out from underneath a stack of papers. You saw the answers to the first three problems and wrote those down when you took the test. You still feel guilty about cheating."

Hannah gasped.

143

Julia burst out laughing.

I closed my eyes again.

"You have a pair of underwear that you consider your 'lucky pair' and you wear them for every basketball game."

This time, both Aya and Julia started laughing.

I continued. "You wish your mom was more involved in your life. You don't feel that she has as close a connection with you as you would like. You resent the fact that she never comes to see you play sports. She doesn't like sports, so she doesn't come. You feel that if she really cared, she'd make an effort to…"

"Stop," Hannah said. "That's enough."

I opened my eyes, "I'm sorry. I'm just repeating what I saw. Was that too personal?"

"Okay, you got me. I've never told anyone any of that."

"Wow," Julia said. "We're believers. You are amazing!"

"Please—don't tell a single soul about this," I said. "I really don't want other people to know."

"Why not?" asked Aya. "I think it's pretty cool! People would be following you around like groupies, wanting to give them a reading or something."

I shook my head. "That's exactly why I don't want people to know. I want to live as normal a life as I possibly can. The stuff about Callie… especially that information, cannot go outside these walls. I'm helping the police and nobody can know about it."

As if on cue, my cell phone rang. I jumped up and dug it out of my pocket.

"Hi, Detective Coalfield," I said.

My friends looked at each other in wonder and then back at me.

"Jenny," he said, "you need to come over to the station."

"Now?"

"Yes, now. I need to give you a little more information about Callie's background. I think it might help you get a little more insight."

"Well, okay…" I said, hesitating. "How long do you think it will take? I'm at a sleepover."

"Oh—not long," he answered. "Maybe a half an hour or so."

"Okay, I'll be right there."

My friends stared at me.

"Either you are a really good actress, or this helping the police stuff is for real!" Julia said in awe. Aya and Hannah nodded in agreement.

"I've got to go for just a little bit," I said.

"Are you going to help the police?"

"Yeah, but he said it wouldn't take very long. Don't start the movie yet—wait for me, ok?"

"We'll wait," Hannah said.

"By the way," I said as I grabbed my purse and headed toward the door, "what movie did you guys get?"

"We got an old Alfred Hitchcock classic. It's called Psycho."

Great.

***

I opened the door to the police station. Detective Coalfield peeked around the corner.

"Ah, there you are," he said. "Come on into the conference room."

I followed him down the hall and into the now familiar conference room. He closed the door behind us.

"What's up?" I asked.

The detective leaned against the windowsill and motioned for me to sit down.

145

"I talked to Callie's parents. It turns out that they lived in southeast Alaska before moving here. A little town called Sitka."

"Alaska?" I asked. "Could that be why I saw the eagle? That actually makes sense."

"The bracelet that you got all of those impressions from—her father bought that for her in Sitka when she was about six years old."

That made sense too. I remembered seeing the islands and hearing the eagles.

"Callie's mom said that after Callie went missing, one of the neighbor kids came by with her bracelet. He found it in the street. She thought that maybe Callie had lost it a while back. But I think it fell off her wrist when the kidnapper grabbed her on the way to the bus stop."

"Then, why did Callie's mom give it to Madeline instead of to the police?" I asked.

"Well, I wish she would have," he remarked. "I don't even think it occurred to her that it was evidence. If she had given it to us, we may have gotten a fingerprint off of it."

I shook my head. "That's too bad… we may have been able to find Callie if you had the fingerprints."

"Maybe, but only if the kidnapper has a prior record, and only if he had touched the bracelet while he was grabbing her," he added. "I asked the Shoemakers if they had any enemies in Alaska."

"And?" I asked.

"And, Mr. Shoemaker used to own a boating tour guide and charter fishing business. He gave us the names of three guys who worked for him over the years that may have been a little disgruntled with him. We're in the process of checking them out."

That sounded pretty encouraging to me.

"Okay," I said, "now what?"

"Now, just keep your mind open. Maybe one of these men will be the guy we are looking for."

"Detective?" I asked.

"Yes?"

"There's something I should tell you …"

"What?"

I explained what happened at the sleepover, including the part where the kidnapper got my name and when he broke Callie's arm.

As soon as I finished, he began pacing the room.

"This changes everything," he said. "We'll have to have someone watching you—you're not safe."

"Are you serious?" I asked. "I can't have a cop following me around school!"

"Well, most likely not at school, but we'll have someone following you to school and after school."

I didn't like it. This was going to affect my social life, and maybe even my dating life. How was I going to explain this to Mike? He might think I would be too high maintenance as a girlfriend if I had a police officer following us around on our dates.

"I know you don't like the idea of it," he said, "but your safety is far more important than what other people think about a cop guarding you."

He had a point, but I still didn't like it.

"I'll follow you back to your sleepover," he said. "If this guy knows who you are, he may have followed you here."

I let out a sigh. "Okay."

I got in my car and drove back to Aya's house, the headlights of Detective Coalfield's car shining my rearview mirror.

Chapter 22

I drove to Factoria Mall, my stomach churning. My date with Mike was just minutes away. My hands shook as I parked my car near the Nordstrom Rack entrance. The police officer assigned to me pulled into a spot a few cars away. We got out of our vehicles, and the officer approached me. He was a pretty big guy, maybe in his early thirties, dark brown hair and eyes.

"Miss, what are your plans here at the mall today?"

"Plans?" I asked. "Why do you need to know my plans?"

"I'm not trying to drive you crazy here. I just want to know which stores you are going to—in case we get separated for some reason. I'm being held accountable for your safety."

"I see. Well, I'm meeting a friend at Red Robin for lunch. After that, I'm not sure. I guess I'll just go home."

"I'll try not to be too obvious. But if you go anywhere else, I'll still need to follow you."

"Okay," I said, feeling a little ticked off. This date was pretty important to me, and I didn't want to feel like I was being watched.

I entered the doors to the mall and looked around near the Red Robin entrance. No Mike. What if he forgot? I was five minutes early, so there was still time. I walked closer to the restaurant and peeked in the windows. I didn't see him anywhere. I started walking a little way into the mall;

maybe he was shopping in one of the stores and lost track of time. I was aware of the police officer following a short distance behind me. Ugh.

Wait. What if he was coming in from the other entrance near Red Robin and I missed him? If he came in there and didn't see me, he might think that I stood him up and then leave.

Turning around abruptly, I headed back to the restaurant. Out of the corner of my eye, I saw the cop shake his head and follow me.

I got back to the Red Robin and peeked in the windows again.

I sucked in my breath as I felt a pair of hands on my shoulders. Someone had come up behind me. It was Mike.

"Hey," he whispered in my ear, "I'm sorry if I scared you."

I turned around, not really knowing what to say. My nerves and skittishness embarrassed me.

The police officer stepped forward.

"Everything okay, miss? Do you know this man?" he asked.

"Yes. He's the friend I'm having lunch with," I squeaked.

"Okay, miss. I'll just be right out here if you need me," he said with a knowing smile.

Drat! Now I'd have to find a way to explain this.

"Jenny?" Mike asked, looking back and forth between the officer and myself. "What's with the cop? What's this all about?"

I looked down at my toes and blew out a sigh.

"Jenny?" He tilted my chin up to meet his gaze.

My insides melted.

I grabbed his hand and led him into the restaurant.

"Come on," I said. "I'll tell you while we eat."

The hostess seated us in a two-person booth in back of the restaurant. It was surprisingly quiet, considering that

149

most days there were multiple families and birthday parties going on in here.

Mike gave me an inquisitive look.

After taking a moment to think about how to explain all of this, I decided that the best tactic was just to tell the truth. If I made something up, we would just be starting a relationship on lies. This way, he could decide right away if he wanted to date a freak or not. The ball would be in his court.

I took a deep breath and told him… everything. The waiter came by several times, took our order, brought our food, but kept the chitchat to a minimum. He could see that we were discussing something important.

When I had finished telling him my story, I took another deep breath and waited.

Mike reached across the table and grabbed my hand.

"Thank you for telling me this."

"I bet you've never dated anyone with so much baggage before, right?" I said nervously.

"Well, there was that girl that had three arms …"

I stared at him; my mouth hanging open.

"Just kidding." His eyes twinkled. Let's just say I've never dated anyone nearly as *interesting* before."

"Interesting! That's a nice way of saying 'weirdo'!"

"No," he said defensively, "I never said 'weirdo'. I don't think you are weird. The circumstances, however, are very, very weird."

"I completely understand if you don't want to have anything to do with me. I wouldn't hold it against you at all."

Mike sat perfectly still. I took his silence to mean that I was too much of a head case for him. I got up and smiled sadly.

"Thanks for lunch," I said. "I'm sorry that it didn't work out."

He stood up and pushed me right back down onto the bench seat.

"Wait, you're not going anywhere," he said. "I listened to your story, now you listen to mine."

My mouth dropped open. His story? Here I was, telling him all about my crazy life, not even considering his past; his story.

He saw the look on my face and reached for my hand again.

"Look, I know that you needed to tell me that stuff. In fact, you don't know how much I appreciate your honesty. But if you think that I'd walk away from you because of what you just told me, well, you're dead wrong."

I blinked.

He went on. "What if you don't like *my* story? What if you don't want to hang around me? My story may not be as dramatic as yours, but maybe it will give you pause before starting a relationship with me."

I couldn't believe this. He actually thought that I wouldn't want to be in a relationship with *him*?

"Well, go ahead," I said. "Please tell me your story."

He sat back, leaning his back against the back of the booth bench.

"Before I moved here, I lived in California. Before that, in New York, before that, in Rome. Before that, in Paris... should I go on?"

"That's a lot of places," I said, wondering where this was all going. "So, why did you move so often?"

He sighed. "My dad has a government job. I'm not even really sure what he does. But we have to move a lot."

"So, what's so bad about that?" I asked, wondering why this was such a big deal for him.

"Well, for me, it was bad. I know it sounds kind of exciting—moving from place to place."

It did sound pretty exciting.

"But imagine being me for a moment. Never being in a place long enough to make friends. Well, at least not long enough to meet good friends. I've never even had a girlfriend for more than a couple of months."

Now I was starting to understand.

"So now it's my senior year. I've had half of it in California and less than half of it here. I have no real connections to anyone. This is supposed to be the best year, but it all feels a little hollow to me."

He looked down at his lap again.

"Until I met you…" he said as he looked up at me.

My heart started pounding harder in my chest.

"When I first saw you and we made eye contact during the auditions… I felt a connection. A real connection."

He looked so sincere. But I just couldn't believe anyone would feel that about *me*.

"Are you doubting me?" he asked, sensing my trepidation.

"No," I said quickly. "I'm just finding it hard to believe that you feel that way about me. We hardly know each other."

"I know it sounds crazy, but the moment I saw you … when I touched you, I felt electric—like there was really good energy between the two of us."

"I felt that too."

He smiled that same smile; the one that melted my heart.

"My parents are secretive about Dad's job and we're moving all the time. I feel like my whole life has been shrouded in secrecy. So, when you just came clean and told me everything; well, that just blew my mind. What I want most out of a relationship is honesty. No secrets."

"No secrets," I repeated.

How ironic. It seemed like my entire life had been a secret. I felt a twinge of regret as I thought about all those years I had kept my gift a secret from my friends and even my family. And now that I was finally telling everyone the truth, that's what Mike found the most attractive about me.

"But aren't you worried that I might put you in danger?" I asked. "This kidnapper guy will most likely come after me, and if you're with me, there's no telling what he might do."

"I'm not worried. I just want to be with you—I want to get to know you better. Besides, maybe if I'm around, that guy won't come after you. I can protect you."

"Do you think your parents might move before you graduate?" I asked, worried that this might all end too soon.

"No—I made them promise me," he said. "I need to stay and graduate here."

I breathed a sigh of relief. "Okay then."

"Okay," he echoed.

"Does that mean you want to go out with me?" I asked.

He took my hand in his. "Yes, I believe it's official then."

Another thought popped into my head. "But you'll be graduating in a couple of months! Are you going to college?"

"Of course I am, but for the first year at least, I'm going to the University of Washington in Seattle. You won't be rid of me that quickly, and even if my parents move again, I'm staying here until I figure out what's next."

I liked the sound of that. He was establishing some roots here on his own terms.

Mike paid the bill and we made our way out of the restaurant.

***

The police officer was waiting outside in the mall. As soon as we emerged from Red Robin, he ambled toward us. I nodded at him, hoping he wouldn't come any closer.

"Where are you parked?" Mike asked.

"I'm parked by Nordstrom Rack," I answered. "How 'bout you?"

"I parked on the other side, by Rite Aid, but I'll walk you to your car."

Mike walked over to the police officer. "If you don't mind, sir, I'd like to walk Jenny to her car. She'll wait for you after I leave. Is that okay?"

"I'll wait here for a few minutes," he said.

"Thanks!" Mike said, smiling as he walked back toward me.

He grabbed my hand and we walked out of the mall and into the parking lot. It was sunny, but cold with a few dark clouds appearing in the west. Mike put his arm around me and led me to my car. When we got to the driver's side, he turned me so that my back was to the door.

"Thanks for coming out to lunch today," he said, brushing the hair away from my face.

"Thanks for inviting me." I suddenly became very nervous. This was one of those awkward moments my friends and I had talked about a million times. One of those "will he kiss you or not" moments.

He tilted my face back up to meet his eyes. "Don't be afraid of me, okay?"

"I'm not afraid! I just—I'm a little nervous. I haven't had many dates," I answered.

"We just need a little time to get used to each other."

He bent down and gently kissed my lips, sending waves of warmth from my head to my toes. I was floored. The kiss was amazing. Better than anything I could ever have imagined.

He pulled away, but I put my hands on his shoulders and kissed him back, letting my lips linger a little longer on his lips. My heart thudded loudly in my chest.

"Wow," he said, smiling. "I haven't been kissed like that in a long time. That was really nice."

He hugged me and then opened my car door. I got in and rolled down the window. He crouched down to talk.

"I just realized," he said, "that I don't have your phone number."

"Oh!" I grabbed my cell phone and handed it to him. "Can you put your number in my contact list? I'll put my info in yours."

He handed me his phone and we added ourselves into each other's contacts lists. He got up out of his crouch and leaned into the car window and gave me a kiss on the cheek.

"See you at school tomorrow," he said with that little grin.

"See you tomorrow." I watched as Mike walked back toward the mall and the police officer came back out.

"Going home, miss?" the officer asked.

"Yes." I sighed. I wished the date with Mike would never end.

Chapter 23

Monday again. When had I ever looked forward to a Monday? Today was different, though. Today I was officially dating a tall, dreamy, talented senior who actually told me on the first date that he felt we had a real connection.

If someone had told me that the sky was falling and London Bridge was falling down, I would've believed them. If someone like Mike could be interested in me, then anything was possible.

Because Mike and I didn't have any classes together, we only saw each other a few times in the hallway. During those times, he would grab my hand or put his arm around me, pulling me close to him.

As we walked down the hall, heads turned and whispering ensued.

"Oh my God! That's Jenny Crumb and that new guy from California! He's pretty hot," I heard as the stream of students filed past us.

Mike heard too. He looked at me and winked—that little grin curling up the sides of his mouth. I felt a little embarrassed to be the center of attention, but proud too.

At the end of the school day, my friends pulled me over to my locker.

"When did this happen?" Julia asked, halfway angry and halfway amused.

I played dumb. "When did *what* happen?"

"Oh, come on!" Hannah punched me playfully on the arm.

"Ouch!" I said, pushing her back. "I don't know what you are talking about."

Aya put her hands on her hips, "Spill it. We want details."

I sighed. "Okay, you got me." They were crowded around me, waiting to hear more. "Mike and I officially became a couple yesterday. I didn't tell you guys because I had no idea that was going to happen."

"What do you mean?" asked Julia. "Did you have a date yesterday? 'Cause you didn't tell us you had a date!"

"I know. I'm really sorry. I meant to, but then all that stuff with the police came up and I kind of forgot to tell you. Will you guys forgive me?"

Hannah shrugged. "Okay, yes, we'll forgive you. But you have to tell us about this guy! Who is he? What's he like?"

"Mike's in the musical with me. He's new here and he's a senior—he lived in California before he came here." I stopped, thinking about what else to tell them.

"I don't think I've seen him," Julia said. "What does he look like?"

Just then, Mike came walking down the hallway. He looked amazing in a light green shirt that matched his eyes and a pair of jeans that accentuated his height.

"He looks like that," I said, pointing down the hall.

All heads turned toward him.

Hannah sucked in her breath. "Whoa … he's…"

"Really hot!" Aya finished her sentence for her.

"Yeah," Julia added dreamily. "Really, really hot."

Mike approached us. "Hey Jenny, are you going to introduce me to your friends?"

157

I made the introductions while my friends silently drooled over him. It was pretty funny watching them fall all over themselves, trying to engage in conversation. Edging over to my locker while they were still talking, I unpacked and repacked my backpack with my homework and other stuff I would need for the theatre.

I rejoined the group and elbowed Mike. "I think we better get to rehearsal… don't want to be late."

"Oh, right. Hey, it was nice meeting all of you," he said, completely oblivious to the starry looks on their faces.

"Bye guys!" I said as Mike and I headed toward the auditorium.

I looked back as the girls mouthed things like, "Oh my God!" and, "You are so lucky," at me.

I giggled and nudged Mike. "Well, you've made quite the impression on them. They seem to really like you."

"You think so?" he asked self-consciously. "I never know what people think about me. Guess I've never been around anyone long enough to find out."

"Well, I can tell you from experience that they like you."

"How can you tell?"

"Are you that oblivious?" I asked incredulously. "They think you're really, really hot."

His eyes opened wide in surprise. "They do?"

I laughed as we entered the auditorium. "Yes. And I think you're hot too." Reaching up on my tip-toes, I kissed his cheek.

Mike turned a bit red and smiled sheepishly. "I guess I didn't pick up on that. That's a little awkward." Then he stopped me and pulled me into a warm hug. "But I'm glad you think so, because I think you are beautiful," he whispered as he kissed me.

Chapter 24

The days flew by with school, homework, and rehearsals. Every night, I had dreams of Callie lying in agony with her broken arm in her cell underground. How could she still be alive? But I was sure that if she were dead, I would somehow know or feel it. The worry I felt for her was torturous. I was torn between wanting to live my wonderful regular life and wanting to go out searching for Callie. I tossed around the idea of driving around neighborhoods in the area, looking for the creepy man's house or the place in the woods where he had buried her. As much as I wanted to find her, my fear and my busy schedule kept me from venturing out to look for her. Of course, had I gone searching, the police officer assigned to watch me that day would surely have kept me from looking for her. Their job was to keep me out of danger.

The police were very good about keeping a low profile when I went to school every morning and when I returned to my car in the afternoon when school was over. Nobody except Mike and I noticed that they were there.

The week of opening night soon arrived. We were scheduled to do two weekends of performances, starting on Friday. That was just one day away. The butterflies in my stomach fluttered around nervously, causing me to drop the notebook I was clutching as I tripped over my own two feet down the hall.

As I bent down to pick it up, I saw my ghost friend, Michelle, standing to the side of the trophy case.

I stood up. "Hi Michelle," I said.

She looked dazed as she turned her head toward me. "Hi … have you seen my boyfriend?"

"You mean, John Cook?" I asked.

"Uh huh," she answered sadly. "I can't find him anywhere."

"Michelle," I said hesitantly, "Uh… I think that… Okay, how do I say this? I think that you should probably know that you're—dead."

Her eyes flashed angrily. "What? You're crazy!"

"No, I'm not crazy. I know it's a shock to you, but it's true."

"Why would you say that to me? What is your problem? You are nuts!" she turned her back to me and disappeared.

I shrugged. I really needed to ask my mom about this girl and what happened to her. I also made a mental note to call Celine and ask her how I should tell a person that they're dead without offending them.

***

Friday.

The morning of opening night. I gathered up my stuff for the day. My mom whisked past me to fill up her coffee cup.

"Mom?" I asked as I zipped up my backpack.

"Mmmmhmmm?" she asked as she sipped her coffee.

"Did you know someone named John Cook and his girlfriend, Michelle, in high school?"

Mom stopped in mid-sip, surprised. Recognition lit up her face.

"Oh yes! I hadn't thought of them in years," she said.

Finally—I was going to find out what happened to Michelle, and why she was a ghost.

"Mom, what happened to them?"

She looked at me suspiciously. "Wait a minute, why are you asking about them? How do you know their names?"

I gave her a knowing look. "Mom …"

"Yes, I almost forgot." She grinned sheepishly. "Have you seen Michelle?" Her face changed to concern.

"Yes. She keeps asking me where her boyfriend, John Cook, is. What happened to her? Why is she dead? Did she die in school?"

"Well, sort of," my mom answered. "She didn't die *at* the school. There was a party at the house of one of her friends. After the party, John was driving them home and there was an accident. Michelle died instantly."

I mulled that over for a second. "And John?" I asked. "What happened to him?"

"He lived," Mom said simply. "He was devastated by her death. After graduation, I never saw him again. Honestly, I don't know anyone who has talked to him since."

Huh. So, he was alive. So then the question became, was I seeing Michelle just because she needed someone to tell her that she was dead? Or should I hunt down John Cook and tell her where he is? Or, did John Cook have something to do with Callie's disappearance and that's why I was seeing Michelle? I was obviously over-analyzing all of this. Maybe she was just a random ghost who had unresolved issues. I really needed to just focus on school and the upcoming performance.

I grabbed my lunch off the kitchen countertop and slung my backpack over my shoulder.

"Mom? Could you find an old yearbook with pictures of John and Michelle?" I asked as I headed for the door. "It would be interesting to see them."

"Sure," she answered. "It will take me some time to dig one up, though. Did I put those in the attic?"

"I don't know," I answered, "but I gotta run!"

I hurried to my car and hopped in. The police officer parked near the house started his vehicle and waited for me to pull out of the driveway.

I looked in the rearview mirror as I drove down my street. In addition to the police car, I saw a shadowy shape slip out behind some large rhododendron bushes. I blinked, but the shape was gone.

Chapter 25

The end of the school day arrived and I was excited and scared to death. The show opened at 7:00 p.m., just a few hours away. Mike was nervous too and we both rushed to our cars to get home and get ready.

He gave me a quick hug in the parking lot.

"Break a leg," he said with a grin.

"You too!"

He opened my car door for me and closed it gently as I settled into the seat. He waved and blew me a kiss as he hurried to his car. I looked in the rearview mirror and I saw the police officer behind me in his car roll his eyes. I laughed and made my way home, wondering if the cop would bust me for speeding if I went any faster.

When I arrived home, I found my dinner on the table with a little note stuck to the plate. "Dad, Jackson, and I will see you at school tonight—Jackson's soccer game runs until 6:00 p.m. I left my yearbook out for you in the family room. Good luck!"

I heated up my dinner in the microwave, got a glass of water and wolfed my food down nervously. Just as I was chewing my last bite, I decided to go grab Mom's yearbook. I got up and retrieved the book and tucked it under my arm as I rinsed off my dishes and put them in the dishwasher.

I ran upstairs and plugged in my curling iron. We were supposed to do our hair before arriving at the theatre.

I quickly did my makeup and sat on my bed with Mom's yearbook, waiting for the curling iron to heat up. I flipped it open and found Michelle's picture. Yup, that was her all right. I flipped through the pages again to find John Cook's picture, and held my breath. Half expecting to see the creepy guy's face as I searched for his name under the photos, I found it.

A handsome guy with dark brown hair and eyes smiled up at me from the pages. He wasn't the creepy guy. Not even close. Huh.

I got up and curled my hair. Thoughts trickled through my brain as I curled. So—what was the deal? I thought for sure this John Cook character had some connection to Callie. So much for being psychic. This whole Michelle and John thing was distracting me from finding Callie's kidnapper.

I unplugged my curling iron and gathered up my things. I grabbed my cell phone, purse, and the yearbook and shoved them into a tote bag.

Just as I was headed out the door, I took the yearbook out one more time. I silently asked God, the Universe, and Angels to help me find the answers to help Callie.

I looked through the pages slowly. As I scanned the photos, my heart stopped. There in the Senior photos… the creepy guy. His name was Richard Grist.

He looked just like he did in my visions except younger. A shudder went up my spine. My adrenaline kicked into gear and I whipped out my cell phone and called Detective Coalfield. I opened my car door, threw my bag in, and started the car.

"Detective Coalfield," he answered.

"I know who he is!" I shouted into the phone.

"Jenny?" he said, alarmed.

"The kidnapper!" I yelled as I backed out of the driveway. My car lurched forward as I stepped on the gas and sped down the street.

"His name is Richard Grist. I found him in my mom's yearbook from 1979. It's him! For sure!"

The police car behind my flashed his lights, warning me to slow down.

"Okay," Detective Coalfield said. "Calm down. I'm running his name right now."

As I drove, images flashed in my mind. I saw a street sign flash as I blinked. "Maple Street!" I said. "He lives on Maple Street!"

"All right," he answered. I could hear him typing and muttering something to someone in his office.

I saw his house… a large piece of property. A path, woods… and another image.

I gasped. "Maple Street in North Bend! She's buried on his property." But before he could respond, my cell phone died. Dead battery.

Trying to control my panic, I drove the last stretch to the high school. I zoomed into a parking space, locked my car, and ran through the doors of the school.

When I got to the theatre, I took my cell phone and charger out of my bag and plugged them into an outlet in the dressing room. I called Detective Coalfield, but my call went directly to his voicemail. I was about to leave a message when the stage manager whisked by, frowning at me.

"You need to get dressed. We only have a few minutes before the curtain opens," he said.

The place was bustling, girls getting dressed and talking excitedly. Actors bumped into me in their hurry to get their costumes and wigs on.

I quickly changed into my costume and found Madeline by the mirrors, putting on a little extra blush.

"Hi!" she said when she saw me. She saw my ashen complexion and she froze.

"What's wrong?" she asked worriedly.

I grabbed her forearms and drew her close. "I know who the kidnapper is—I just told your dad."

I could see the different emotions flit across her face. Excitement at the prospect of finding Callie, but horror and fear as well.

"Oh my God," she breathed.

I searched her face. "What should we do?"

She swallowed. "Well, we let my dad do his job, and now we have to do ours. We are going to go out on that stage and knock 'em dead. And, oh my God... he could find Callie tonight! I can't believe it!"

She tried to smile bravely. I echoed her tentative smile.

She collected the blush and a brush off the counter with her trembling hands. "You look really pale," she said as she swished some color on my cheeks.

"I'm not sure that any amount of blush will change that," I said with a nervous laugh. "Between the excitement of opening night and the prospect of finding Callie, I think all the color has drained out of my body!"

Madeline put the blush down. "We are going to be awesome tonight! And my dad will find Callie—it's all going to work out!"

I said a silent prayer, hoping she was right about that.

***

The curtain opened. I couldn't see the clapping audience, as the lights were bright on stage and my eyes hadn't had a chance to adjust.

The music began. It was surreal. Once we started, I was in another world and having the best time I've ever had. The crowd laughed in all the right places and cheered wildly after almost every song.

During the first act, I managed to catch a glimpse of my family. They were sitting in the middle section about halfway back. Jackson was watching the play intently and looked almost proud.

Then came intermission. The cast was hyper with excitement. Ms. Nakamura patted us on the back, saying, "Great job, everyone! Keep up the good work."

When the curtain opened for the second act, the energy from the cast and the audience made me giddy. This was so much better than cheerleading. I wanted to do this for the rest of my life.

In the play, the Baker's Wife gets killed by the giantess who was searching for Jack. Jack had killed the giantess's husband earlier on in the play, and she was seeking vengeance for his death. So, when we got to that part, I was kind of sad, because I wouldn't be appearing back onstage for a song or two, until I came back to sing my farewell—as a ghost, to the Baker and my baby son. The stage crew had done a great job creating a giant foot that came out from backstage and appeared to crush me.

The audience gasped as I fell to the stage and lay lifeless. I really wanted to see the expressions on their faces, so I cracked my eyelids open just a millimeter.

My view was of the front row. And sitting directly in front, dead center, was Richard Grist. The creepy guy.

A bead of sweat trickled down the side of his face. He had his rapt attention right on me, a grin spreading across his face.

The stage lights went dark and I got up to exit the stage. My heart was hammering in my chest. My body shook as I ran to the dressing room and just as I reached for the cell phone, it rang. It was Celine.

"Jenny!" she said, "Listen to me—you're in danger!"

"I know," I said in a raspy whisper, "He's here! He's in the front row!"

"You've got to get out of there," she instructed. "Hurry!"

"I can't!" I answered. "I still have to go back on stage."

A beep interrupted her. "I've got another call," I looked at the number. "It's Detective Coalfield."

"Take the call, but get out of there as soon as you can," she said.

"Okay," I clicked the green button, "Detective?"

"Jenny," he said, "we've got Callie."

"Oh my God! How is she?"

"She's injured and in a lot of pain, but she's alive."

"That's great!" I said, so relieved that she had made it.

"But listen, Detective, he's here!"

"What?" he said, his voice tinny in my ear.

"He's here! Richard Grist is here!"

The connection broke, I looked at my cell phone in disbelief. I heard my cue and ran back on stage. As I ran, I prayed that he had heard me, that he knew to send the police here.

On stage, I sang my farewell song to the Baker … to Mike. I realized how much he meant to me. He was everything I could ever hope for in a guy. I smiled at him and choked back a tear. As I sang my last note, I bravely looked into the front row, ready to look the kidnapper in the eye and meet my fear head on.

But he was gone.

***

The cast sang our curtain call song together, holding hands. Mike held my hand warmly and squeezed. I squeezed back—a little too hard and he gazed at me with a curious expression. I looked up at him, worry tearing through my stomach. The audience, oblivious to my feelings, clapped and cheered, giving us a standing ovation. Mom, Dad, and even Jackson were whooping and grinning.

168

The curtain closed and he wrapped his arm around me.

"What's wrong?" he asked as he led me off into the wings.

"The kidnapper is here," I whispered. "But now I can't see him anymore—I'm scared."

Mike looked completely shocked.

"Here?" he asked.

I saw movement in the wings—the area on stage right that opened into the green room. As we walked past the black curtains, the hair on the back of my neck stood up. The rest of the cast had already moved into the green room, talking excitedly as the applause lingered on in the auditorium.

"Yes, he's …"

Someone grabbed me from behind, wrenching me away from Mike.

"Scream and you're dead," the man hissed in my ear.

Mike shouted, "Hey! Let go of her!"

The man's arm snaked toward him. I saw a glint of silver as he stabbed Mike in the chest. Mike sucked in his breath and doubled over.

"Mike!" I screeched. "No!"

The man covered my mouth with his hand. "Shut up or I'll kill you too."

I struggled and tried to scream, but then he spat into my ear. "I know where you live. Scream and I'll kill your entire family."

I stopped struggling, but managed to twist around. Mike was lying on the floor, his hand to his chest. Blood was trickling out between his fingers. He glanced up at me, his face a mask of pain and horror. Oh God, please don't let him die.

Why wasn't anyone coming to help? The audience was still clapping—maybe there was too much noise to hear what had happened. Richard Grist dragged me away toward the exit. Just as he pushed open the door and threw

169

me into the night, I heard a shout. I hoped that someone had found Mike. Hot tears streamed down my face. This wasn't happening … was it?

He pushed me through the door and dragged me to his car, close to the exit. I had always heard that you should never let an attacker take you in a car—never to the next destination, as it could be your last.

A single word popped into my head: stall.

"Mmmmmm… mmmm," I struggled to say.

"What?" he asked, annoyed with me. "I told you what would happen if you screamed."

He dragged me closer to the car.

"Mmmmmm… mmmmm …"

"If I move my hand off your mouth and you scream, I'll kill you," he threatened.

I nodded.

He removed his hand from my mouth and turned me to face him.

The moon illuminated his pale face. His honey colored eyes glowed menacingly in the night. His entire being emanated evil.

"Uh," I cleared my throat. Think… think… what should I say? Please God, help me think of something.

"You're wasting my time," he hissed and reached out to put his hand on my mouth again.

An idea popped into my head. I didn't know where it came from, but it was good.

"You went to school with Michelle," I blurted out.

He looked confused. "Michelle?" His eyes darted around nervously.

"And John Cook," I said quickly.

He gave me a suspicious look. "John Cook? What— where did you hear about them?"

"It doesn't matter where I heard. How did Michelle die? Were you responsible?" I asked. I had no idea where the thought came from, but I went with it.

He sneered. "Ha! That was my first one," he said proudly. "It was genius, really. I asked her out and she laughed at me—in front of her friends. She humiliated me."

I gave him a sympathetic look. "That must have been awful."

"And that stupid boyfriend of hers—he threatened me. Told me I had to stay away from her or else he and his sidekicks would beat me up." He grinned. "Nobody tells me what to do."

"I can see that," I said, trying to keep my voice steady and calm. "So what did you do?"

"I followed them to their little party and while they were having a fun time laughing about me with their friends, I cut the brakes on John's car." He smirked. "I wish I could have seen their faces when they realized they couldn't stop."

Sirens wailed in the distance.

"Hey!" He grabbed me and spun me around. "You're just like the others," he breathed in my ear. "You pretend to like me and then you try to sell me out. Do you think you're clever?"

He jabbed the knife point into my throat.

"Huh? I *said*, do you think you're clever?" He poked the tip into the skin on my neck. I winced as a warm trickle of blood ran down my collarbone.

"No, I don't think I'm clever. I was just interested in you."

He snorted. "Yeah, right."

Over his shoulder, I watched as the door we'd come out of opened ever so slightly. A cop. The same one that had escorted me to the mall on the first date I had with Mike. His eyes opened wide in surprise. He pulled his gun.

Richard turned his head to follow my gaze. Suddenly, he yanked me toward him and spun me around to face the police officer. He stood behind me, holding me with one arm, the knife at my neck.

"Take one more step," he warned the officer, "and I'll slice her from ear to ear."

His attention was so focused on the cop, that his reaction was too slow as I took a quick step forward and thrust my right leg backward, catching him in the crotch. He doubled over and groaned. I lunged away from him but he grabbed my ankle and pulled hard. Gasping, I fell face-first onto the cold pavement.

The cop seized the opportunity and moved straight toward us. "Stop! Drop the knife!"

I looked back at Richard Grist. His diabolical face contorted with anger, and he sneered at me. With a heart-stopping screech, he catapulted himself on top of my body. I closed my eyes, waiting for the moment when he would plunge the knife through my back.

No. I couldn't give up. I had to fight. Anger swelled inside me, and with it came renewed strength. I reached my arm around to his leg, and dug my fingernails in.

"Bitch!"

"Now!" I screamed. The officer shot… the retort of the gun ringing in my ears.

The impact sent Richard Grist toppling over and onto the pavement. I turned to see if I was clear of him. A red hole in his forehead glistened in the moonlight, his eyes glazing over.

Sirens, flashing lights, police cars, and the wail of an ambulance sounded as I lost consciousness.

***

I woke up on the way to the hospital. "Mike?" I muttered.

"Shhhhh…" the paramedic riding with me said in a soothing tone. "Just rest."

I closed my eyes, but didn't fall asleep or lose consciousness again.

The ambulance rumbled over the road. It slowed and turned around a corner. After it stopped, the doors opened and the paramedics wheeled me out on my stretcher. Back to the hospital again, I thought with a sigh.

"Hey," I said to one of the paramedics, "I'm okay. I can walk."

"Not until you get checked out by a doctor."

"Fine," I muttered under my breath, only wanting to see Mike.

They wheeled me into the emergency room. Another stretcher was being rolled in ahead of me with great speed. The paramedics were running. A news van pulled up into the emergency parking lot—the crew poured out of the van, cameras at the ready.

Through the crowd of people, I caught a glimpse of the stretcher, long legs horizontal, brown hair.

"Mike?" I called out. "Mike!" I tried to sit up.

One of the paramedics gently pushed me back down into a prone position.

"Shhh, Miss … you need to rest," he said.

They wheeled me in and took me into a curtained area. A young woman with a white doctor's coat flipped open the curtain and approached me.

"Hi," she said, "I'm Dr. Andrews, and you are?"

"Jenny Crumb," I answered. I didn't want to stick around and answer stupid questions. I just wanted to find out what had happened to Mike.

"Okay, Jenny," she said, "I'm going to check you over and see if you're all right."

"I'm fine, really I am," I said as I sat up.

She took a look at my throat, "Hmmm. There's a little blood here."

She reached over to the table by the wall and pulled out a cotton ball and poured a little clear liquid on it from a bottle nearby. She swabbed the area and got out a bandage.

"What happened," she asked as she unwrapped the band aid. She placed it on my neck.

"Uh… a deranged man held me hostage by knifepoint after he stabbed my boyfriend," I answered matter-of-factly.

Her eyebrows shot up. "The guy with the knife wound is your boyfriend?" she asked.

"Yeah, and I *really* need to see him," I said as I scooted off the stretcher. "Is he all right?"

"Is this the only injury you have?" she asked as she gently sat me down on the edge of the stretcher.

I pushed her arm aside. "Yes, as I said earlier, I'm fine. Please, let me see Mike."

She reluctantly led me down the hall to the emergency waiting room. My family was there talking to another family. Everyone's eyes were red-rimmed—they'd been crying.

They turned to look at me coming down the hall with the doctor.

My parents rushed toward me. "Oh my God! Jenny! You're alive!"

They hugged me and kissed me. Even Jackson seemed happy to see me. I looked over their shoulders at the other family.

"Is that Mike's family?" I asked.

"Yes, dear. It is." Mom said.

I broke loose from my mom and dad and approached them.

"Hi," I said, looking into their dazed faces. "I'm Jenny. I'm Mike's girlfriend."

His mom touched my arm. "He's told us so much about you."

"Have you seen him yet?" I asked cautiously. I wanted to ask if he was dead or alive, but I couldn't do it.

"No," his dad answered, as he blew out a breath. "They said a doctor is coming down to talk to us in a bit. We don't know anything yet."

As if on cue, a doctor came through the double doors at the end of the hall. "Mr. and Mrs. Kramer?"

His mom and dad rushed forward.

The doctor looked grim. "Your son has had a very bad injury, a stab wound to the chest. He's lost a lot of blood."

Mike's mom was shaking and crying. His dad was holding on to her, trying to keep her standing upright.

The doctor looked back and forth between his mom and dad. "It's really touch and go. If he makes it through the night, then he has a chance of surviving. But I really can't say quite yet."

His mom burst into tears and her knees gave out. Mike's dad helped her up and wrapped his arms around her. Oh God. This was all my fault. I wish he'd never been interested in me. He would be fine if he hadn't tried to protect me. My heart sank and I began trembling. Mom and Dad rushed over to me and led me to a chair.

I heard the doctor saying, "We need to take him into emergency surgery and put in a chest tube to drain the blood ... will you sign the papers?"

Blinking back the tear, I watched as the doctor led them over to the emergency room desk and they began the paperwork.

Detective Coalfield rushed through the sliding glass doors at the entrance to the ER. His eyes met mine and he ran over to me. My dad got up from his chair and motioned for the detective to sit down.

"Jenny! Are you all right? My men told me what happened. I can't believe that guy actually had the balls to show up at your performance!"

175

"I'm fine, but my friend, Mike—my boyfriend…" Tears welled up in my eyes. "He might not make it."

He put his arm around me. "I'm sorry, honey," he said. "I hope he makes it. But you have to know, you saved Callie. You saved her life."

I sniffed. "How is she?"

"She's okay. Or at least as okay as she can be considering what she's been through. She's here in the hospital. You can go visit her tomorrow or the next day if you want."

"I'm going to stay right here until I find out about Mike," I said resolutely.

"Okay," he said looking up at my parents. "If you want, you can take your son home and I'll stay here with her."

Mom and Dad looked at me, they seemed unsure.

"It's okay," I said. "Why don't you guys go get some sleep. Jackson looks so tired." Jackson really did look tired, and scared. It was the first time he'd ever been this silent.

They looked at each other, debating. "Well, Mom said. "Call us the minute you hear anything. One of us will come be by your side."

"Okay," I said.

I watched them walk out the sliding glass doors. Mike's family came back and sat in the chairs near us. For the first time that evening, I looked down at myself. I was still wearing my costume. I looked like the Baker's Wife. I didn't think the Baker was wearing his costume anymore. He was probably wearing a hospital gown, and it was my fault.

It was my fault that Mike was near death, and it was my "gift" that put him there. But then again, it was my gift that saved Callie's life.

My eyelids felt heavy. Now that my adrenaline surge was over, I felt so very tired all of a sudden. So tired.

Maybe if I just closed my eyes for a little while, I could have the strength to get through this.

Callie's dad was talking to Richard Grist. They were standing on a dock.

"Rich, I have this great idea for a Fathometer for my charter fishing boats," he said enthusiastically. "I know you have an engineering degree. Would you consider building a prototype for me? If it works, it could make you and me very rich. This thing would not only tell how far the terrain is below you, it would show the fish and tell you how big and what type of fish they are—maybe even show a 3D image. I've got a long list of features that would make this thing amazing. There is nothing on the market like this currently. What do you say?"

"Just give me your list of features. I'll do it."

There was a flash ahead to a future point in time. The men were sitting in a small cramped office.

"Here it is," Richard said as he presented it to Callie's dad.

"Richard, this is great! Let's get this onboard to install it."

The two men walked down the dock.

"So, Jim, we haven't really talked about payment…"

"Oh, yeah, that's no problem. We'll get it worked out." Jim climbed onboard the fishing vessel. "Can you hand it to me?"

"Thanks," he said as he reached toward it.

Richard hesitantly held out the Fathometer, and then pulled it back. "Not so fast, Jim. I want to discuss payment for my design."

Jim looked surprised. "Oh, of course! I'll have my lawyer put together a contract… how 'bout 50/50?"

Richard chuckled, his eyes glinting. "I don't think so, Jim. I'll take 60/40, with me getting the 60 percent, naturally."

Jim looked confused and then shocked. "But this was my idea. It's my business. And I've already paid you for the time you spent working on it."

Richard's eyes sparked dangerously. "Your idea would be nothing without my expertise. Make it 80/20."

"I'm sorry, Richard, but that's just not going to happen. I'm happy paying you a fair cut, but…"

Richard exploded in anger. He yelled profanities, jumped on the boat, and started smashing everything he could get his hands on.

Jim jumped off the boat. "Stop right now. If you don't, I'll have to call the police. Be reasonable, Richard—this is my idea and my business!"

"Your business?" hissed Richard. "Who cares if it's your business? I built the damn thing!" He snatched up the Fathometer and hurled it against the side of the boat, where it broke into several pieces. "Look what you made me do!" he screamed. "You idiot! Now you have nothing! Nothing! You'll pay for this!"

My eyes flew open. I blinked. I was still in the emergency room waiting area. Mike's parents had fallen asleep in their seats.

The detective was leaning back in his chair and noticed I was awake. "Jenny?" he murmured. "What is it? Are you okay?"

I think I know why Richard Grist took Callie." I explained the dream to him.

Detective Coalfield shook his head in disbelief. "Boy, that guy really knew how to hold a grudge. Ten years or so, and then he takes Jim's daughter?"

Flash.
A redhead.
A blonde.
Three brunettes.
More girls.

178

There were others. He didn't just hold a grudge against Jim.

"Oh my God!" I said quietly.

"What?" he asked.

"I think there were others," I said. "Callie is not the only girl he took."

Flash.

Building boxes.

Shoveling dirt.

Burying in the ground.

Screams.

Clawing to get out.

"Detective, you should really check into all the missing girls in the area. Dig up his property."

He sat upright and looked alarmed. He took his cell phone out of his pocket and walked down the hall.

Several news crews complete with camera guys blew past him and approached me.

"Miss—are you Jenny Crumb? Were you held hostage by the crazed man in the parking lot of Newport High School?"

"What can you tell us about this man? Did he hurt you?"

I was dazed, surrounded by microphones, cameras, and reporters.

"Uh…" I stammered.

Just then, the doctor from last night came through the double doors. He approached the news crews. "We need a little privacy right now. I'll be out in about ten minutes to talk with you folks… preferably outside."

The reporters looked disappointed, but also hopeful. They headed out the door to the parking lot to wait for the doctor's statement.

Mike's parents stood during the frenzy and waited for the doctor. As he walked toward them a look of sheer dread clouded their faces.

179

I held my breath, preparing for the worst.

"He made it," the doctor said to all of us. "We're moving him to the ICU right now."

Mike's parents embraced each other. I jumped up and ran to hug them.

"Now, it's going to be a long recovery, but I think he'll be all right."

"Can we see him?" his mom asked anxiously.

"As soon as they settle him into his room upstairs," the doctor said. "Give us an hour or so. Why don't you go up to the cafeteria and get something to eat?"

Food sounded good right about now—even hospital food.

Detective Coalfield came back and we told him that Mike had pulled through. "That's the best news I've heard in a long while!" he said with a grin. We started toward the elevators. "Jenny—I've got my men scouring Grist's property right now. They'll call me if they find anything."

***

When we got the go-ahead to see Mike, his parents went in first. Detective Coalfield and I sat outside the room, letting them have some time with him alone. I called my parents and filled them in. They said they would pick me up soon.

After about a half hour, Mike's family came out. "Go on in and say hello to him. We told the staff it was okay for you to visit. He's groggy, but he's awake." They sat down in the chairs in the hall and I went in, a little scared.

His bed was raised at a slight incline—there were tubes peeking out of his hospital gown in his chest area. Even though his face was ashen, he was still incredibly handsome. My Mike.

I walked over to his side, held his hand, and looked into his green eyes. I had never been so glad to see him. "Oh, Mike—I…"

"I know, Jenny," he said, his voice choked with emotion. "God, I'm so glad to see you."

He looked away for a moment. "I'm so sorry I couldn't protect you. I feel like I let you down."

I swallowed my tears, "No, I'm sorry! You didn't let me down!" I urged. "You got hurt because of me. You almost…"

I couldn't say it. He almost died for me.

He looked up at me. "But I didn't. I didn't die. I'm not going anywhere."

I leaned in to kiss his cheek. He closed his eyes for a moment. He looked so tired.

"So…" He opened his eyes and searched my face. "Nobody told me what happened. How did you get away? What happened to that creep? Did he hurt you?"

"No," I stroked his hand, "he didn't hurt me— although, if he had gotten me into his car, he surely would have." I described the rest of the events that had taken place after he was stabbed.

"He's dead?" Mike asked.

"Yes, very dead. He can't hurt anyone ever again. And by the way," I added, "Callie is alive. In fact, she's in this hospital. I'm going to go visit her before I go home."

"Let me know how she is," he said and closed his eyes again.

I patted his hand. "I'm going to let you rest, okay?"

"Okay," he murmured sleepily.

I caressed his cheek, and then squeezed his hand.

"Thank you, God," I whispered.

I walked to the door and turned to wave, but he was already asleep.

***

Upstairs, I walked toward Callie's room with Detective Coalfield. A nurse came out of her room.

"Oh!" she said as she saw us coming. "Are you here to see Callie? Are you family?"

Detective Coalfield explained, showing her his badge.

"Go right in. She already has a visitor in there, though."

We opened a door and saw Madeline standing by Callie's bedside.

"Dad!" She threw herself into his arms. Then she hugged me. "Jenny! You're all right! I was so worried!'

"How did you get here, pumpkin?" Detective Coalfield asked.

"Mom drove me, of course," she answered. She went back to Callie's bedside.

Callie was lying in bed with her arm bandaged up. She looked horrible. She was swollen everywhere, like she'd been beaten up really badly. I tried not to let my horror show on my face.

She chuckled a little. "I look pretty bad, don't I?"

I went to her side. "Uh, no—you look... okay... you look pretty bad. I'm sorry," I said apologetically.

She laughed. "It's okay. I guess I look as bad as I feel. But you know what? I'm alive."

I peeked at her broken arm. "How were you able to keep going? I didn't think you could survive being held captive for so long."

"I'm alive because of you. Madeline told me everything. If it weren't for you, I'd still be buried underground." She shuddered at the memory of it.

I patted her good arm. "It must have been horrible. I'm so sorry. You're going to be okay, though. Madeline sure is a good friend to you—she wouldn't let up until I figured out where you were."

She looked at her friend with admiration. "That's my Madeline!"

Madeline patted Callie's shoulder affectionately. "Hey, speaking of looking kind of bad, Jenny—you look really tired, and you're still in your costume. You should go home and get some rest."

"I think I might do that."

I waved as I left the room. Dad was standing out in the hall talking with Detective Coalfield. He hugged me and gave me a kiss on the cheek.

"Come on, Jenny, let's go home."

"Wait." Detective Coalfield said. "You were right about Richard Grist having more victims. We've found at least six bodies buried near the chamber that he locked Callie in."

I nodded solemnly. I had figured as much.

"I'm sure that the parents of these girls will be very glad to have some closure," he said.

Not when they found out the kind of torture they had endured.

Chapter 26

I slept for a long time. It must have been one o'clock in the afternoon the next day before I even lifted my head from the pillow. When I woke up, I knew what I had to do. I shuffled into the office and opened my laptop.

I typed "John Cook" into the search engine and pulled up a long list of John Cooks. I closed my eyes and said a little prayer. "Please God, let me find the right John Cook." When I opened them, I was immediately drawn to one entry in Wenatchee. I scribbled down the address on a sticky note and went downstairs.

Mom was in the kitchen making a pot of something delicious.

"Mmmm… that smells really good," I said as I made my way to the coffee pot. "What are you cooking?"

Mom gave me a side arm hug as she lifted the lid to show me. "My famous chili," she said. "There's cornbread in the oven. I thought you might like a little comfort food today."

"That's great! I could probably eat the whole pot. I'm starving!"

Mom laughed. "What's new?"

"How long does it take to drive to Wenatchee?" I asked as I opened the cupboard, taking out a bowl and small plate.

"Wenatchee? About two and a half to three hours," she said, furrowing her brow. "Why do you want to drive to Wenatchee?"

"You'd better sit down," I said as I put on an oven mitt and took out the cornbread. "It's kind of a long story."

I told her every detail of the night before, including the part about Michelle and her boyfriend, John Cook.

"Whoa!" my mom said, her hands flying up to her mouth in shock. "Richard Grist caused the accident that killed Michelle?"

"That was the first girl he killed, and I'm afraid he killed many more after her."

"What? I can't believe it. I barely remember Richard from high school. He was so quiet. I do remember him being teased a little though."

"I think he got teased quite a lot," I said. "It seems as though he chose to hold a grudge against everyone who ever crossed him. He was a bomb waiting to go off."

"So, why did you ask how far a drive it is to Wenatchee?" my mom asked.

"I found John Cook through the internet. He lives in Wenatchee." I sighed. "Mom, I think that Michelle needs to move on. You know, to the other side."

Mom raised her eyebrows. "What are you planning to do about it?"

"I have a rough idea of what to do." I explained my plan.

"Get your jacket," she said. "We're going for a long ride."

***

When we found the dirt road that John lived on, we looked at each other nervously.

"Do you think he'll go along with it?" Mom asked.

185

I shrugged. "I have no idea, but I think it's worth a try."

We turned down his road, lined with apple trees. The sign by the main road said, "Cook's Organic Apple Orchards, .25 miles."

"He went from a football star to an apple farmer," Mom said quietly.

"What's wrong with that?" I answered as our car jerked up and down with the potholes.

"Oh nothing, of course," Mom said quickly as she held on to the wheel and tried to steer us around the potholes. "It just surprises me that a guy like him would be working on a farm. I thought he'd become a politician or a doctor or something."

"Maybe he just likes the quiet country life," I suggested.

"Are you kidding? He was the life of the party in high school. He was definitely a people person."

We arrived at the end of the road, where a modest farmhouse stood. There was a mid-90's pickup truck in the driveway, and we scooted in next to it. I glanced nervously at my mom and then got out of the car.

"Well, here we are!" I said, trying to sound at ease.

Mom got out of the driver's side.

"Shall we knock?" she said as she motioned toward the door.

"Huh? Oh yeah… okay," I said as I walked up the little path to the red door.

I rang the doorbell. Nothing. I knocked gently on the door. Nothing. Great. I hadn't planned on him not being there. I couldn't believe we had driven all that way for nothing.

I turned around in a huff and was about ready to cry when I spotted something in the grove of apple trees. Someone was sitting on a small yard tractor in between the row of trees. He was hunched over the tractor controls with some tools seemingly oblivious to the visitors in his driveway.

A smile crept across my face and I mouthed the words, "There he is," to my mom.

She turned her head to follow my gaze.

We walked through the apple trees toward John. His concentration and attention to his work finally broke when he heard the soft tamp of our shoes on the dirt road.

He looked up in surprise. "Can I help you with something? Are you lost?"

He was still a handsome man. He looked like his yearbook picture except that his face had filled out a little more and was lined from working out in the sun.

I realized that I didn't know what to say now that I was standing in front of him. Mom sensed my apprehension and stepped forward, extending out her hand to shake his.

"Hi, John," Mom said confidently. "My name is Mary Crumb—my maiden name is Parker. Perhaps you remember me from high school?"

"High school?" He smiled warmly. "Mary Parker... Mary Parker... You were in my English Composition class, right?"

"Yes, I think I had a couple of other classes with you as well. And, I watched you play many a football game."

"Great to see you, Mary!" But then a perplexed look emerged on his face. "So, what brings you out here? Do you live around here now?"

She shook her head. "No, my daughter here... uh..."

Now she was at a loss for words and I took over.

"Hi, I'm Jenny," I said. "It's kind of a long story why we're here. I met a friend of yours, an old girlfriend."

"Really?" he said in surprise. "An old girlfriend? I..."

"Actually, John, I met Michelle—your girlfriend from high school."

His whole demeanor changed from warm and friendly to angry and defensive.

"Is this some kind of sick joke?" he bellowed. "Do you think this is funny?"

I took a step back. Mom took a step forward and put her arm in front of me, trying to shield me from his anger.

"Whoa, whoa, whoa!" she said protectively. "This is no joke. My daughter has a gift. She…"

I gently pushed my mom's arm down and stepped forward. "John, I'm psychic."

A look of shock crept over his face. "What?"

"I know that this sounds crazy," I explained, the words just tumbling out. "But I'm a student at Newport High School. *Your* high school. Michelle's high school. And I'm telling you, I see her almost every single day. She paces the hallway looking for *you*."

His body seemed to deflate and his anger disappeared.

"Michelle's looking for me? That would mean that…"

"That Michelle's a ghost," I answered. "She hasn't made it to the other side. She's confused and doesn't realize she's dead."

"Oh my God," he said quietly. "I can't believe this."

"Trust me," I said, "It's true. It's so sad to watch her day in and day out, wandering the halls, looking for you. But I think I know how we can help her. We can help her get to the other side."

He sat down on his tractor seat and slumped over.

"Michelle was the only girl I ever really loved. When she died, my whole world fell apart." He sighed and wiped the sweat from his brow. "You know, Michelle's not the only one who hasn't moved on. After the accident, I finished high school, went to college, and put one foot in front of the other. I never got married—avoided serious relationships like the plague. I just never got over her, you know?"

"There's something you should know," I said quietly. "The accident was no accident."

He looked up in shock. "What do you mean?"

"Do you remember Richard Grist?" I asked.

"Richard Grist? No. Who is he?"

"He went to school with you," I said.

"I don't remember him."

"He was pretty nerdy," Mom said. "Lots of kids teased him. He made a pass at Michelle, remember? Everyone was laughing about it."

"Oh, yeah! That guy!" he said. "He was a real piece of work."

"You have no idea."

"Huh?" he asked.

"Richard Grist cut the brakes on your car while you and Michelle were at a party. The party you attended on the night of the accident."

John sat in stunned silence.

"No, that can't be," he muttered.

"It's true. Richard Grist caused the accident. He killed Michelle."

He suddenly came to life and jumped out of the tractor seat. "That bastard! I'll kill him!"

I stepped toward him and grabbed his arms. "You don't have to do that. He's already dead."

I explained Callie's kidnapping, my visions, and the final minutes of Richard Grist's life.

He shook his head in disbelief. "I spent my whole life feeling responsible for Michelle's death. The idea that this Richard Grist person purposefully killed her... it's unbelievable."

"So, John?" I asked gently. "Will you help Michelle? Will you help her find peace?"

He sat still for a moment, looking down at the ground. "I'll do whatever it takes."

Chapter 27

I sipped the hot tea and sighed as I sat back in Celine's comfortable antique arm chair. It was Sunday evening. It was amazing to think that I could have been dead two days earlier.

"So," she said as she plopped a cube of sugar in her tea cup and stirred. "Have you started to come to terms with your gift? Have you accepted it?"

"I guess I have. I mean, I can see how powerful it is to be able to help people. But, I'm a little worried about my future."

Celine raised her eyebrows in surprise. "Your future?"

"Well, no offense, but I can't really see myself doing what you're doing. Don't get me wrong, it's wonderful what you do." I could feel myself blushing, worried that I may have offended her. "What I mean is, what you do is amazing. You help people all day long and then you go out and teach other people to develop their gifts so they can also help other people. It's really great."

"But, you don't think you want to do what I do? Is that what you're saying?" she asked.

"Yes, I guess that's what I'm saying," I said. I fidgeted with my tea cup and looked down at my lap.

"Jenny, to help people, you don't have to have a little psychic hut with a sign out front advertising tarot card readings, palm readings, or whatever."

I looked up. "I don't?"

"No!" Her musical laughter drifted around my ears and resonated through my heart. "It doesn't matter what you choose to do for a living, you can help people anywhere at any time. It's not a conscious thing. You can sense other people's sadness, right? If you feel that they want to reach out to someone, let them reach out to you. It doesn't matter if it's a stranger sitting on a park bench, lonely and needing to talk, or if it's a dear friend who needs some good advice. You will instinctively know what to say to help them."

I smiled, relieved that I wasn't obligated to do this for a living.

"Do you have any ideas as to what you might want to do as a career?" she asked.

"I guess I really like acting and singing," I answered. "But now that I've worked with Detective Coalfield, I kind of like the idea of getting some really awful people off of the streets; so, maybe forensics or profiling."

"Either way," she said, "your gift will lead you to help others. Helping others is your calling, not necessarily any one career in particular. Go with what will make you happy."

I hadn't made up my mind which career path I would choose, but it was comforting to know that I could choose any job I wanted.

I thought about Richard Grist—about how he chose to hurt people wherever he went.

"Don't worry about Richard Grist," Celine said, picking up on my thoughts. "He is what's called a Black Soul, and he won't be bothering you for a while."

"A Black Soul? What does that mean?"

"A Black Soul is a person that has turned their back on God a long time ago," she answered.

"You mean, like an atheist?"

"Oh no!" she chuckled. "Atheists are people who are just confused about the existence of God."

"So what happens to atheists when they die?" I asked.

"Trust me," she answered, "they are just very surprised when they cross over and find themselves on the Other Side surrounded by old friends, loved ones, and God."

"So Black Souls…"

"They are souls who know that God exists, but they have intentionally decided that they want nothing to do with him. When they die, they are immediately reincarnated and have to live yet another miserable life. Unfortunately, the rest of us have to deal with them over and over again."

"Only people with black souls are reincarnated?" I asked, confused.

"No, most of us have lived many lives, but we *choose* to come back. We choose to live our lives here to become better souls. This is our school. This is the way we learn how to become better human beings—compassionate and loving. Those who are Black Souls don't have a choice. They have to come back whether they want to or not. This is their own hell—here on Earth. Yes, they make our lives miserable when we come in contact with them, but they live with far more misery than we could ever imagine."

"Do they go on like this forever then?" I asked.

"No, I don't think so. Eventually God will forgive them and enfold them back into his loving energy. But that may take centuries. I don't really know."

"Wow." I said quietly. "So, now I have another question."

"Go on," she said.

"If someone has died and they are stuck here, how would I help them get to the other side?"

Chapter 28

On Monday, I went to school, but it felt so empty without Mike.

"Why the sad face?" Julia said as I got out my books for the next class.

"Well, for obvious reasons, I guess," I said.

"At least Mike is doing okay. School is almost out for the summer and there are a lot of things to look forward to."

"Always the eternal optimist." I gave her a hug.

"Well, I've gotta jet! I have a test next period," she said and hurried away.

"Good luck!" I called after her.

I walked down the hall and turned the corner. I saw Madeline get to her next class and I waved as she went through the door. She waved back.

I guess I had to follow Julia's lead and look for the good things that had happened this year. I had found a new friend, I had met the boy of my dreams, and I had finally done something with my gift. Saving someone's life was no small feat. Maybe just being myself wasn't such a bad thing.

***

The next Saturday, John met me at the high school. I knew that the doors would be open because we would be having a performance in the evening with another guy, Scott Hames, playing Mike's role. They were rehearsing with the new guy in the morning. I would be joining the rehearsal in an hour or so.

I had spent the days before the weekend going to school and visiting Mike every evening until they kicked me out. He was getting stronger and looking less pale each day. I read him books, played cards, and watched TV with him. Now that the weekend was here, I knew that I had to focus on this unfinished piece of business, and I was scared that I wouldn't get it right. What if Michelle disappeared when I brought John in? What if she didn't recognize him?

There were news vans out in the parking lot. I suppose they were trying to get more footage of the area where the shooting happened. From what I had heard, they still weren't quite sure why Richard Grist had tried to kidnap me. So far, they were speculating that he was obsessed with girls who were in the drama program. I was a little bit worried that perhaps someone would say something about me being psychic. I didn't think my friends would rat me out, but sometimes information like that could leak out unintentionally.

"This sure doesn't look like the school I remember," John said as we stepped into the Commons area.

"I bet! They remodeled a few years ago."

We walked down the hall and I stopped as I spotted her by the trophy case.

"There she is," I said. "Stay here for a minute—let me go talk to her."

He looked around nervously. "All right."

I walked down the hall and approached her as she paced.

"Have you seen my boyfriend?" she asked me.

194

"Actually, I have seen your boyfriend, Michelle."

She stopped pacing and looked at me. "You have?"

"Yes, I have," I answered. I turned and motioned for him to join us.

She watched him approach.

"John?" she asked. "Is that you?"

John looked around and waited for me to say something.

"John?" She wrinkled up her nose. "You look different... older."

"He can't hear you, Michelle," I said.

"He can't hear me? Is something wrong with him?" she asked.

"No, nothing's wrong," I answered.

"Are you talking to her?" John asked. "What is she saying?"

"She doesn't understand why you can't hear her," I explained.

"Why can he hear you, but not me?" she asked frantically.

"John! John!" she said, reaching for him.

He shivered, wrapping his arms around himself.

I turned to her. "Michelle, do you remember the accident?"

"Accident? What are you talking about?" she asked. "Why can't he hear me? Can he see me?"

"No, he can't see you and he can't hear you because ... you're dead. Remember? We talked about this before?"

"I'm not dead!" she yelled angrily. "I'm not!"

"You and John went to a party, do you remember that?" I pressed on gently.

"Party? The party at Janet's house? I remember."

"Do you remember what happened after the party?" I asked.

"Uh... we left."

"Yes, you left in his car, and then what happened?"

195

She hesitated. "I… I don't remember."

I nudge John and whispered. "Tell her what happened."

"Michelle—it's me, John. We were in the car and it was dark. Do you remember? We were approaching a curve on the road, so I put my foot on the brake, but the car didn't slow down. The brakes didn't work. I was able to keep on the road for about a mile more, but then there were more curves ahead. We crashed. I was injured, but you were…" He choked back his tears. "You didn't make it, Michelle. You died there at the scene of the accident."

She stared at him, in shock. She turned to me for confirmation. I nodded to her that what John was saying was true.

"Dead?" she asked.

"Yes."

I heard a noise next to me and looked at him. Tears were streaming down his face and he was shaking.

"Michelle, if you can hear me… please. I'm so sorry this happened. You were the love of my life." His eyes watered.

I reached into my pocket and handed him a crumpled up tissue. He took it gratefully. He wiped his eyes and cheeks.

"I don't think either of us has moved on," he whispered. "I know I haven't. I never got married, Michelle. It was so hard. I guess I never got over you."

She seemed deeply touched by his words.

"So…" he wiped his cheeks again. "So, maybe it's better if we do move on. We've both suffered enough."

"How?" Michelle asked. "How do I move on? What am I supposed to do?"

"Do you see a white light anywhere?" I asked, thinking that it sounded awfully cliché and stupid. "A tunnel or something like that?"

Michelle turned around slowly, "Oh, I think I do see a light, way over there. That's strange. Wonder why I never saw that before?"

"I think it's because you weren't looking for it," I answered.

She hesitated, and turned toward John again. "I love you, John," she said.

And before I could tell him what she said, he answered with, "I love you too, Michelle. I'm sure I'll see you again someday."

She turned and walked slowly to the light. Looking back over her shoulder, she smiled, and waved goodbye.

"Thank you," she said as she disappeared.

"I can't believe that just happened." John raked his fingers through his hair. "Was that real?"

"It takes some getting used to," I said.

"Now what?"

"What do you mean?" I asked.

"What am I supposed to do now that I've let her go?"

"I guess you're supposed to live your life. I don't think Michelle would want you to be pining after her for the rest of your life, would she?" I squeezed his arm. "She'd want you to be happy."

"I suppose she would." We turned and walked down the hall. Out in the parking lot, I hugged him goodbye, and he got into his truck and drove away.

I felt good. Finally, I felt truly grateful for my gift. I had helped two people today, John and Michelle. And I had saved Callie's life. Now it was time for me to move on with *my* life. The school year was coming to an end, and barring any other crazy events, I had the whole lazy summer ahead of me.

About the Author

Martina Dalton writes young adult fiction and lives in the Pacific Northwest with her family. Born and raised in Alaska, she can nimbly catch a fish, dress for rain, and know what to do when encountering a grizzly bear. Now living in the Seattle area, she uses those same skills to navigate through rush-hour traffic.

When she's not writing, she hangs out here: https://www.facebook.com/AuthorMartinaDalton

Coming in October 2013
The Sixth Sense of Jenny Crumb
Book Two in the Jenny Crumb Series

4848220R00111

Made in the USA
San Bernardino, CA
12 October 2013